Dorm Room 2B or Not 2B
Copyright © 2025 by Dylan Roxi
All rights reserved.

Book Cover and formatting provided by Trisha Fuentes
https://bit.ly/m/trishafuentes

No part of this book may be reproduced in any form or by any electronic or mechanical means, including information storage and retrieval systems, without written permission from the author, except for the use of brief quotations in a book review.

ISBN: 979-8-3492-3356-2 (Paperback)

Published by
Ardent Artist Books
www.ardentartistbooks.com

About Ardent Artist Books

➥ ABOUT US

Ardent Artist Books was established in 2008
We publish modern and historical romances once a month!

Get Your FREE List: Published & Upcoming Books
visit our website at:
https://bit.ly/3Wva4o0

* * *

➥ WE HAVE BOOK TRAILERS

Follow us on YouTube!
https://bit.ly/3W3xn7a

* * *

➥ **WE HAVE SERIALIZED FICTION!**

Visit our website today to download one of our stories that unfold in bite-sized pieces!

Each installment is just 99¢!
Paperback $15.99

https://bit.ly/3LsDpJL

Dorm Room 2B OR NOT 2B

A BWWM BEST FRIENDS BROTHER ROMANCE

Dylan Roxi

Contents

1.	Dorm Room 2B	1
2.	It's My Life	21
3.	Varying Temperatures	39
4.	Random Moments	59
5.	A Leather Wallet	77
6.	Channeling	95
7.	Thanksgiving Day	117
8.	What the Fuck?	135
9.	#HookupNow	153
10.	Out For A Drink	171
11.	No Personal Questions	191
12.	Real Names Only	209
13.	Whatever This Is	223
14.	Best Part of Me	239
15.	Like a Physical Blow	257
16.	Run From Love	279
	Acknowledgments	297

You Might Also Like

Love Child - Part 1	301
Love Child - Part 2	303

New for 2025

Paris Fling	307
About Dylan	309
Also by Dylan	311

ONE

Dorm Room 2B

WHITNEY BARNES

I SHOVE another stack of textbooks aside on our cluttered center table, creating just enough space for the takeout containers Quinn's about to drop there. Our dorm room—a tiny two-bed that we somehow made home after freshman year—looks like a bomb went off in a theater department storage closet. Scripts, highlighters, and costume pieces litter every surface.

"You're a lifesaver," I say as Quinn balances the Chinese food in one hand while kicking the front door closed with her foot.

"Figured we'd need brain food for this study marathon." She tosses her blonde hair over her shoulder and plops down on our secondhand couch, which sags precariously in the middle. "I'd rather die than fail Professor Whitman's scene study exam."

I snort, grabbing the container of lo mein. "Dramatic as always."

"Hello? Drama major?" Quinn rolls her eyes but grins, her perfect teeth flashing white against her glossy pink lip gloss. "It's literally in the job description."

That's my roommate in a nutshell. Quinn Hunter—gorgeous, charismatic, and allergic to actual studying. We met during freshman orientation when we both auditioned for the same student production. She forgot half her monologue but still charmed the directors with her megawatt smile and natural stage presence. I nailed my lines but got the supporting role. Somehow, instead of becoming rivals, we became inseparable.

"Speaking of drama," Quinn says around a mouthful of sweet and sour chicken, "you'll never guess who I saw at that party on Grove Street."

"Who?" I twirl noodles around my fork, already knowing whatever gossip she has is way more interesting than memorizing these lines.

"Tyler Jenkins." She wiggles her eyebrows suggestively. "And he was asking about me."

"Basketball Tyler or saxophone Tyler?"

"Basketball, obviously." Quinn tosses a fortune cookie at me. "He's got those hands, Whit. You know what they say about guys with big hands."

I catch the cookie with surprising dexterity. "That they wear large gloves?"

"You're impossible." She laughs, tucking her legs underneath her. "Anyway, he asked for my number, and I'm pretty sure he's gonna text me this weekend about that frat party."

"What happened to that guy from your Psych class? The one with the dimples?" I ask, trying to keep track of Quinn's revolving door of admirers.

"Oh, Ethan?" She waves dismissively. "Too nice. Called me to make sure I got home safe after our coffee date. Who does that?"

"A decent human being?"

"A *boring* human being." Quinn reaches for her phone as it buzzes. "I need excitement, passion! I need a guy who makes me feel like I'm in one of those movies where the girl gets pushed up against a wall."

I nearly choke on my lo mein, my mind instantly flashing to last Friday night. Jax's hands gripping my hips, his mouth hot on my neck, my back against his apartment door the moment it closed behind us. The memory sends a flush of heat through my body.

"You okay there?" Quinn asks, her eyes narrowing slightly.

I cough, reaching for my water. "Wrong pipe."

She studies me for a second longer before returning to her phone, thumbs tapping away at lightning speed. "Anyway, Tyler's definitely more my speed. Those athletes know what they're doing, you know?"

"Mmm," I hum noncommittally, desperate to change the subject. "Shouldn't we be running lines instead of discussing your love life?"

"God, you're such a buzzkill sometimes." Quinn tosses her phone aside and dramatically flops back on the couch. "Fine. But first—why don't you ever talk about who *you're* seeing?"

My stomach tightens. "Because I'm not seeing anyone."

"Bullshit." She sits up straight, suddenly laser-focused. This is the Quinn that directors love—when she turns on her intensity, it's impossible to look away. "You disappeared last weekend for like twelve hours. And the weekend before that. You're seeing *someone*."

I busy myself with organizing the scripts on the table. "I was at the library, then that audition for the independent film."

"The audition was two hours, max. And nobody spends ten hours at the library on a Friday night unless they're hooking up with someone in the stacks." She narrows her eyes. "Is it Professor Hendrick's TA? That guy with the man-bun who always stares at you?"

"What? No!"

"Then who?" She leans forward, green eyes sparkling with curiosity.

For a split second, I consider telling her about Jax. About how we matched on that dating app three months ago. How we agreed to keep things casual—just hookups, no strings attached. No real names, no personal details, no messy emotions. Just mind-blowing sex whenever our schedules align. It's perfect for both of us—I don't have time for a relationship with classes, rehearsals, and auditions. He's got his own busy life he's vague about.

But something stops me. Maybe because Quinn can't keep a secret to save her life. Or maybe because what Jax and I have feels like mine alone—the one part of my life that's just for me.

"There's nobody," I insist, grabbing my script and waving it in her face. "Now, are we going to pass this exam or what?"

Quinn groans but reaches for her own heavily highlighted script. "Fine. But this conversation isn't over."

"Page forty-two," I say, ignoring her comment. "You start."

She clears her throat dramatically and transforms before my eyes. This is one thing I genuinely admire about Quinn—for all her laziness with memorization, when she actually performs, she's electric.

"'How dare you come back here after what you did?'" she reads, suddenly embodying the betrayed lover the scene calls for.

I slip into character, letting Whitney Barnes fade into the background. "'I had no choice. You know I would never have left if—'"

Quinn's phone buzzes again.

"Sorry!" She breaks character instantly, diving for her phone. "It might be Tyler."

I sigh, letting my script fall into my lap. "Quinn, the exam is *tomorrow*."

"It's him!" She squeals, completely ignoring me. "He wants to grab coffee after his practice! Should I say yes right away or wait twenty minutes?"

"Maybe focus on not failing first?"

She pouts, her perfectly glossed lower lip jutting out. "Just because you're determined to graduate summa cum whatever doesn't mean the rest of us can't have a life."

"I want to have a career, not just a degree," I say, trying to keep the edge out of my voice. "You know how hard it is for Black women to break into serious acting. I need every advantage."

Quinn's expression softens. "You're already amazing, Whit. You're going to be accepting your Oscar while I'm still doing local car dealership commercials."

I laugh despite my frustration. "Hey, don't knock commercials. Steady paychecks."

"*Exactly* my plan." She grins, tossing her golden hair. "I'll be the pretty face selling whatever while waiting for my rich husband to come along. Not all of us have your talent or ambition."

"You do have talent," I insist, because it's true. "You just need to—"

"Work harder, memorize my lines, take it seriously." She waves her hand dismissively. "I know, I know. But seriously, some people are meant for greatness—like *you*. And some people are meant to look pretty and have fun —like *me*."

I want to argue, to push her to see her own potential, but I've had this conversation with Quinn too many times before. Instead, I check my own phone out of habit and feel that familiar flutter when I see a text notification.

> Jax: Free tomorrow night?

My pulse quickens, and I quickly turn my phone face-down on the couch beside me, hoping Quinn didn't notice.

"So... back to the scene?" I suggest, picking up my script again.

Quinn squints at me suspiciously. "Who just texted you? Your face did that thing."

"What thing?"

"That thing where you try not to smile but you totally are on the inside." She lunges for my phone, but I'm faster, snatching it away.

"It's just an audition notification," I lie.

"Bullshit." Quinn crosses her arms. "I bet it's a guy. I can always tell when it's a guy."

I force a laugh. "Can we please just rehearse? I'll help you with your lines."

"Fine." She sighs dramatically. "But only because I know you'll eventually crack and tell me everything. You always do."

Except this time I haven't. And I don't plan to. Jax is *my* secret—the one thing that's just for me. Sometimes I think about what it might be like to have more with him—to know his real name, his story, who he is beyond those intense hazel eyes, and the way his hands feel on my skin. But then I remember our rules, the simplicity of what we have.

"Okay, from the top." I straighten my posture and try to focus on the scene, not on when I might see Jax again. "'I had no choice. You know I would never have left if—'"

"Do you think I should wear that blue top or the green dress for coffee with Tyler?" Quinn interrupts, already scrolling through photos on her phone.

I let my head fall back against the couch with a groan. At this rate, we'll both fail tomorrow's exam, and I'll have to kiss my GPA goodbye. But as Quinn starts holding up different earring options to her webcam for my opinion, I can't help but smile. This is college life with Quinn Hunter—chaotic, distracting, and never, ever boring.

Quinn's script falls to the floor as she lunges for her buzzing phone again. I check the time—we've been "studying" for forty-five minutes and gotten through exactly three pages. At this rate, we'll both flunk spectacularly tomorrow.

"Tyler says his practice might run late." She frowns at her screen. "Do you think that's code for 'I'm not that interested'?"

"Or it could be code for 'basketball practice actually runs late.'" I flip a page in my script, trying to focus on the next scene. "Can we please just—"

"He sent a sweaty gym selfie!" Quinn squeals, thrusting her phone in my face. I catch a glimpse of chiseled abs before she yanks it back to type a response. "What do I say? Is 'looking good' too basic? Should I be more flirty?"

"Quinn." I tap her script with my highlighter. "Exam. Tomorrow. Career-defining moment?"

"Don't be dramatic." She rolls her eyes. "It's just one exam."

"Says the drama major."

"Exactly! It's all about performance, not memorization." She tosses her hair over her shoulder. "I'll wing it tomorrow. I always do."

"And how did that work out for you last semester with Professor Mitchell?" I raise an eyebrow, referring to the time Quinn forgot half her lines during our final scene and had to improvise by pretending her character had a stroke.

"I passed, didn't I?"

"With a D-minus."

"Still a passing grade!" She grins triumphantly before her phone buzzes again. "Ooh, he responded to my response!"

I fight the urge to grab her phone and toss it out our second-story window. Instead, I return to my lines, trying to focus on the emotional resonance of the scene, the subtext beneath the dialogue. This is what I love about acting—finding the truth within the words, building a character from the inside out. When I'm on stage or in front of a camera, I'm not just reciting lines; I'm living them.

My phone vibrates beside me, the screen lighting up.

> Jax: If no response means yes 9pm?

Quinn's head snaps up at the sound. Like a predator sensing weakness, her eyes lock onto my phone. "Someone's popular tonight."

I casually flip my phone over. "Just a notification."

"Uh-huh." She gives me a knowing look. "Your phone's been buzzing all night too."

"It's nothing."

"Nothing doesn't make you blush like that." She points an accusatory finger at my cheeks, which I can feel warming treacherously. "Spill it, Barnes. Who's texting you?"

My mind races for a convincing lie. "It's—it's just this guy from the football team."

Quinn's eyes widen, and I immediately regret my choice of cover story. Football players are very much in her social orbit.

"Which one?" she demands, sitting upright, all thoughts of Tyler temporarily forgotten.

"Um..." My mind frantically searches for a name that won't get me caught. "Mike...Johnson?"

"Mike Johnson?" Quinn repeats slowly, her brow furrowing. "Defensive tackle, Mike Johnson? The one with the neck tattoo?"

Crap. I have no idea if there's even a *Mike Johnson* on the team.

"No, not him," I backtrack quickly. "The other Mike. Mike... Williams?"

Quinn's suspicious expression melts into excitement. "Oh my God, Mike Williams the wide receiver? Whitney! He's like, top NFL draft pick material! When did this happen? How? Why didn't you tell me?"

The genuine enthusiasm in her voice makes me feel

guilty for lying, but I'm in too deep now. "It's really new. We just started texting. Nothing serious."

"Is he asking you out? What does he want? Let me see!" She makes another grab for my phone, but I clutch it to my chest.

"No! I mean, it's private. We're just getting to know each other."

Quinn falls back against the couch, eyes wide. "This explains so much. The disappearing acts, the secret smiles at your phone..." She gasps dramatically. "Have you hooked up with him already?"

The irony isn't lost on me. I am hooking up with someone—just not Mike the Imaginary Football Player.

"No, nothing like that," I lie, thinking about Jax's hands on my skin last weekend, how he'd pinned my wrists above my head while trailing kisses down my neck. "Like I said, we're just texting."

"You have to let me help you with this," Quinn declares, completely abandoning her script now. "Mike Williams is serious boyfriend material. Not just hook-up material. He's got NIL deals already! His Instagram has like fifty thousand followers!"

I squirm under her intensity. "I don't need help, Quinn. Can we please focus on the exam?"

"This is way more important than some stupid exam." She waves dismissively. "What are you going to wear when you see him? Please tell me you weren't planning on those ripped jeans and that old sweater you love."

"There's nothing wrong with my sweater," I mutter defensively. "And we don't have plans to meet up yet."

My phone buzzes again in my hand. Quinn's eyes light up.

"Is that him? What's he saying? Let me help you draft a response."

I glance down quickly.

> Jax: I've been thinking about how you tasted all week

Heat flushes through my body, and I quickly lock my screen before Quinn can see. There's no way I'm sharing this with her.

"Just confirming the time," I lie smoothly.

"Time for what?"

"Study group. For my theater history class." The lies are piling up, but I can't stop now. "Tomorrow afternoon."

Quinn pouts, clearly disappointed it's not her imaginary football connection. "You should suggest meeting for coffee. Somewhere public but intimate."

"I'll think about it," I say, desperate to change the subject. "Now, scene forty-two, page three?"

"I still can't believe you've been talking to Mike Williams and didn't tell me." She shakes her head in disbelief. "I thought we shared everything."

The guilt twists in my stomach. Quinn and I do share almost everything. Our apartment, our clothes (though she borrows mine more than I borrow hers), our dreams and fears and embarrassing stories. But Jax—he's different. He's my secret escape from everything: school pressure, audition rejections, Quinn's chaos. When I'm with him, I'm not Whitney the responsible student or Whitney the aspiring actress or Whitney the reliable roommate. I'm just Nikki, the woman he can't keep his hands off.

"It's not a big deal," I say quietly. "Really."

"If you say so." Quinn doesn't look convinced. Her phone buzzes again. "Tyler wants to know if I'm free after coffee tomorrow to 'hang out.'" She makes air quotes. "That means sex, right?"

"Probably," I admit, grateful for the subject change.

"I should make him work for it." She taps her chin thoughtfully. "But those abs..." She looks back at her phone, considering. "I'll tell him maybe. Keep him guessing."

My phone vibrates again. Quinn raises an eyebrow.

"Your 'study group' seems pretty active tonight."

I ignore her comment and check my message.

> Jax: Last time was good. Next time will be better. I've got plans for you.

I bite my lip, my body responding instantly to his words. With Jax, it's always like this—raw, primal chemistry that defies rational thought. I should respond, but not with Quinn watching my every move.

"So, scene forty-two?" I try again, picking up my highlighted script.

Quinn sighs dramatically but finally relents. "Fine. But this conversation isn't over. I want all the details about Mike."

"There are no details to share," I insist truthfully, since Mike doesn't exist.

"Yet," she adds with a sly smile. "Want me to casually mention to Tyler that you think his teammate is cute?"

"No!" I say too quickly. "I mean, I'd rather let things develop naturally."

"Whatever you say," Quinn shrugs, finally picking up her script. "But when you and Mike Williams become official, remember who called it first."

She starts reading her lines, and I try to focus on the scene, but my mind keeps drifting to Jax's message. Tomorrow night, 9 PM. The anticipation is already building, that delicious tension that comes with knowing exactly what's going to happen when we're alone together.

For now, I'll play along with Quinn's excitement about my fake football player. I'll study for this exam and help her pass, too. I'll be Whitney Barnes, dedicated student and supportive roommate.

But tomorrow night, I'll slip away and become Nikki again. I'll lose myself in Jax's arms, in his bed, in the fantasy we've created together. No names, no backstories, no complications.

Just for a few hours, I'll escape from everything else—even my white lie about Mike Williams, which I'll have to untangle eventually.

But that's tomorrow's problem. Tonight, I just need to get through this scene study with Quinn, ignore the buzzing of my phone, and try not to think about what Jax's "plans" might entail.

"'How could you possibly understand what I've been through?'" Quinn reads dramatically, finally focusing on her script.

I take a deep breath and slip back into character, pushing thoughts of Jax temporarily aside. "'Maybe I understand more than you think...'"

TWO

It's My Life

WHITNEY BARNES

I SQUINT at my reflection in the foggy bathroom mirror, wiping away condensation with the back of my hand. The shower's hot steam has turned our tiny bathroom into a sauna, making my curls spring up in tighter coils around my face.

"Get it together, Whitney," I mutter, dabbing concealer under my eyes to hide the evidence of another late-night memorizing lines.

Quinn's already bolted for her 8 AM class—how she manages to look Instagram-ready that early is beyond me. Meanwhile, I'm still trying to make myself look human before my 10 AM Shakespeare workshop.

My phone buzzes on the counter, making me jump. I expect it to be Jax, but instead, my mother's name flashes across the screen. A text this time, not another call I can ignore.

> Mama: Have you thought about what we discussed? The business program application deadline is next Friday.

I set the phone face-down with more force than necessary. The conversation from two nights ago replays in my head like a bad movie I can't turn off.

"Whitney, darling," Mama had said in that honey-sweet tone that always precedes something I don't want to hear. "I just don't understand why you're throwing away your potential on something so... unpredictable."

I'd been half-listening while highlighting my lines for class, phone tucked between my ear and shoulder. "Mama, we've been over this. Acting isn't a hobby for me."

"You got a 1480 on your SATs. You could transfer to any business program in the country. Your cousin Janelle just started her MBA at Wharton, and she—"

"I'm not Janelle," I'd cut in, the familiar frustration rising. "I don't want to spend my life in boardrooms discussing quarterly projections."

"At least you'd have a life you could count on! This acting business... baby, do you know how many talented Black women are fighting for those same few roles?"

That's when I'd tuned out, letting her words wash over me like they always do. The statistics. The odds. The backup plan speech.

Now, as I blend my foundation, I can still hear her voice. *"I just want security for you. Is that so wrong?"*

Maybe it isn't wrong, but it isn't my dream. My dream is seeing my name in lights, hearing an audience fall silent when I step onto a stage, making people feel something real in a world of filtered fakery.

I practice my smile in the mirror, the one that says *I've got this all figured out*. It doesn't quite reach my eyes.

My phone buzzes again, and this time when I glance down, it's him.

> Jax: Last night was fire. Round 2 tonight?

My heart does that stupid little flutter thing it's not supposed to do with a hookup. Three simple words: *"Last night was fire."* They shouldn't make me feel this warm rush, this surge of something that feels dangerously close to pride. But they do.

I pick up my phone, thumbs hovering over the keyboard. What should I say? Playing it cool is getting harder. I'm supposed to be "Nikki" to him—confident, carefree, no-strings-attached Nikki who doesn't count the hours between messages or memorize the pattern of freckles across his shoulders.

The eyeliner pencil trembles slightly in my hand as I lean toward the mirror. Focus, Whitney. I trace a delicate wing on each eye, trying to ground myself in the routine.

Jax is like some addictive substance my body craves. The way his hazel eyes crinkle when he laughs. The way his blonde hair falls across his forehead when he hovers over me. The way he knows exactly where to touch, when to be gentle, when not to be.

Three nights ago, wrapped in his sheets, my head on his chest listening to his heartbeat slow, I caught myself thinking dangerous thoughts. *What if we met for coffee instead of just between sheets? What if I told him my real name?*

But that would break our unspoken rules. No real names. No real connections. No real chance of real heartbreak.

I set down the eyeliner and grab my mascara. The familiar ritual calms me: open, swirl, apply. My lashes darken and lengthen with each stroke.

My phone lights up again. Another text...

> Jax: You there, Nikki? Don't leave me hanging

I should be focusing on my audition piece for the spring showcase. Professor Winters hinted there'd be industry scouts attending. This could be my break—the one that proves to my mother that this path wasn't a mistake.

But instead, I'm thinking about how Jax's hands feel tangled in my hair, how his lips taste like mint and whiskey, how he whispers things against my skin that make me forget my own name—my real name, not the fake one I gave him.

I pick up my phone again, my thumbs typing before my brain can catch up.

> Whitney: Busy tonight. Deadlines.

I hit send, immediately regretting how cold it sounds. But before I can type something softer, more Nikki-like, my phone chimes with his response.

> Jax: Tomorrow then. I can be patient when the reward is worth it.

My stomach does a little flip. This is dangerous. The way I look forward to his messages. The way I've started cataloging things throughout my day to tell him before remembering we don't do that. We don't share our days, just our nights.

I finish applying my lipstick—a deep berry shade that makes my brown skin glow. The girl in the mirror looks confident, put-together. No one would guess she's being pulled in so many directions she might snap.

Mama wants the sensible daughter with the business degree and 401(k). My professors want the dedicated student who lives and breathes the craft. Quinn wants the fun roommate who's always up for adventures and late-night talks.

And what does Jax want? Just Nikki. The girl who doesn't exist outside his apartment.

I glance at my watch and curse under my breath. If I don't hurry, I'll be late for class, and Professor Winters has a strict lockout policy.

Tossing my makeup into my bag, I try to refocus on the day ahead. I have my Shakespeare monologue to perform, lunch with the drama club to discuss the showcase, and then an evening rehearsal for the student-directed one-act I landed a supporting role in.

No time for Jax. No time for my mother's disappointment. Just the steady march toward a future I can almost taste—bright lights, applause, validation.

But as I grab my phone to tuck it into my pocket, I find myself typing one more message.

> Whitney: Tomorrow works. Your place at 8?

The rush of anticipation after I hit send is embarrassing. I should be this excited about my audition, not about sneaking away to a hookup's apartment.

Still, I can't deny the truth as I gather my things and head for the door: if I could choose between a night mastering my craft and a night in Jax's arms, I'm not sure which would win.

There's ambition burning in my veins—the kind that wakes me up at night with visions of success so vivid they feel like memories from a future already written. But there's also this other thing, this pull toward someone who only knows a fraction of who I am.

I lock the bathroom door behind me and scan our small dorm apartment. Quinn has left her usual hurricane of clothes and textbooks in her wake. Coffee cups litter the counter, and her laptop sits open on the couch, the screen dark but waiting. For a moment, I envy her certainty—the easy way she moves through life, taking what she wants without questioning if she deserves it.

My phone buzzes in my hand. Jax again.

> Jax: Cool, I'll kick Ryder out. Bring that thing you wore last time. You know the one.

I feel heat rise to my cheeks, remembering exactly which "thing" he means. Not sure that lacy black number even qualifies as clothing.

I should be focused on becoming the next Viola Davis, not sexting with a guy whose last name I don't even know. But here I am, grinning at my phone like an idiot, already planning what I'll wear tomorrow night.

My ambition and Jax—they're both pulling at me, demanding my attention, my energy. One is my future, my dream, the thing I've worked toward since I was old enough to recognize power in performance. The other is just right now, just tonight, just temporary.

At least, that's what I keep telling myself.

* * *

I SLUMP LOWER in my uncomfortable lecture hall seat, clicking my pen against my notebook in a silent rhythm. Professor Winters drones at the front of the room, gesturing dramatically at a projection of what looks like a 16th-century stage diagram. His voice rises and falls with practiced theatricality, but his words dissolve before they reach me.

"...and Shakespeare's understanding of sightlines was revolutionary for the time period..."

My notebook page remains stubbornly blank where my notes should be. Instead, the margins have become a garden of abstract swirls and tiny stars. I've drawn a miniature curtain in the corner, complete with tassels and folds. Next to it, I've sketched eyes—Jax's eyes, though I refuse to acknowledge that even to myself.

Someone coughs two rows ahead. The fluorescent lights flicker once, twice. Outside the window, a group of freshmen laugh as they cross the quad, their carefree smiles making me feel unexpectedly old.

"Ms. Barnes?"

I jolt upright, my pen skittering across the page.

"Would you care to enlighten us with your thoughts on the symbolism in Ophelia's mad scene?" Professor Winters' eyebrows arch over his wire-rimmed glasses.

Shit. I haven't been paying attention for the last fifteen minutes. My mind scrambles for something—anything—intelligent to say about Hamlet. *What was the question again?* Ophelia. Mad scene. Symbolism.

"Well," I begin, straightening my shoulders, "Ophelia's distribution of flowers represents her fractured mental state, but also serves as her final act of agency in a world where men have stripped her of all power. The rue she keeps for herself symbolizes her regret, while—"

"Yes, thank you, Ms. Barnes." Professor Winters nods, seeming satisfied enough to move on to his next victim. "Mr. Daniels, would you add anything?"

I exhale slowly, silently thanking my high school English teacher for drilling Shakespearean symbolism into my head. Crisis averted.

But my mind immediately drifts back to more pressing concerns than Ophelia's botanical choices. The rehearsal this afternoon. The showcase audition. Professor Winters' offhand comment last week still rings in my ears: "Only five students will be selected for the Broadway Workshop Program."

The Broadway Workshop.

Just thinking about it sends electricity through my veins. Five students. All expenses paid. Three days in New York. Masterclasses with Tony Award winners. Performances attended by casting directors who matter. People who could change everything with a single business card passed across a cocktail table.

I flip to a fresh page in my notebook and force myself to focus, writing "REHEARSAL NOTES" at the top in all caps.

My role in "Glass Menageries Reimagined" isn't huge—I'm playing Laura in Cara Davidson's experimental adaptation that sets Tennessee Williams' classic in 2023 Harlem—but Professor Winters will be watching. He's one of three faculty members selecting those five lucky students.

I need to nail this. Need to make him see me as more than just another drama major with stars in her eyes.

My pen starts moving again, but instead of notes about Shakespeare, I'm jotting down character motivations for Laura. Modern Laura. ***My*** Laura.

Laura's disability = anxiety disorder? Social media trauma?
Glass animals = digital avatars she creates?
Gentleman caller = influencer she idolizes?

The ideas flow faster than I can capture them. This is where I come alive—in the creation, in the becoming. Not in lecture halls discussing dead playwrights, but in the electric space where text transforms into life.

If I can just show Professor Winters that I understand Laura—really understand her—maybe he'll see that I deserve one of those five spots.

Mama's voice creeps into my thoughts. *"And then what, Whitney? You get a taste of New York, get your hopes up, and then what?"*

I push her voice away. I can't afford doubt. Not today.

A memory from last week's rehearsal surfaces—Cara's frustrated sigh when I hesitated during a pivotal moment. "You're holding back, Whitney. Laura's fragility shouldn't make her small. Find the power in her vulnerability."

Find the power in vulnerability. I roll the phrase around in my mind, wondering how someone does that. Power and vulnerability feel like opposing forces

—like trying to stand firm while also allowing yourself to fall.

Like trying to keep things casual with Jax while also counting the hours until I see him again.

No. Not going there.

I draw a thick line under my Laura notes and force my attention back to Professor Winters, who's now discussing the political implications of Hamlet's indecision. Fifteen more minutes. I can focus for fifteen more minutes.

But my mind betrays me, slipping sideways again. The rehearsal space—that converted warehouse the drama department leases off-campus—materializes in my thoughts. The unforgiving fluorescent lights. The floor marked with colored tape indicating different stage configurations. The smell of coffee and desperation.

I need to arrive early. Run my lines again. Work on that moment in Scene Three where Laura shows her collection to Jim. Find that elusive sweet spot between fragility and power.

A notification lights up my phone screen face-down on my desk. I flip it over quickly, hoping it's not visible to Professor Winters.

> Quinn: Did you grab my boots? The black ones with silver buckles? Need them for improv class!!!

I type back quickly:

> Whitney: No, check under your bed

Another text immediately follows.

> Quinn: Already did! Not there! EMERGENCY!!!

I sigh. Quinn's definition of "emergency" could use some recalibration. But before I can respond, another text pops up.

> Jax: Thinking about last night. That thing you did with your—

I slam my phone face-down so fast it makes a loud clapping sound against the desk. Several heads turn. Professor Winters pauses mid-sentence, eyebrows raised in my direction again.

"Sorry," I mouth, feeling heat flood my face.

Great. Just great. Now I'm blushing in Shakespeare class because my hookup decided to text me inappropriate things at 10:45 AM on a Tuesday.

I need to focus. The Broadway Workshop. Laura. Glass animals. Vulnerability with power.

I take a deep breath and try to center myself, scribbling more character notes to ground my thoughts.

> *Laura's connection to her digital creations = escape from reality*
> *Her limp = psychological rather than physical?*
> *How does she move through space when uncomfortable vs. comfortable?*

The movement question sparks something. I've been playing Laura as constantly hesitant, constantly shrinking. But what if her physical presence changes depending on her environment? Small and protective in the outside world, but expansive and confident in her own created spaces?

Yes. That's it. That's the key I've been missing.

"...and with that, we'll conclude for today," Professor Winters announces, closing his laptop. "Remember, two-page response papers on the use of metatheatrical elements in Hamlet are due Friday."

The usual shuffle of bags and chatter erupts around me. I gather my things slowly, still turning over my

Laura-epiphany when Professor Winters calls my name.

"Ms. Barnes, a moment?"

My heart lurches. *Did I miss something important? Is he going to call me out for not paying attention?*

"Yes, Professor?" My voice comes out steadier than I feel.

He adjusts his glasses, studying me with that penetrating gaze that makes students either worship him or fear him. "Your monologue last week. Cleopatra's death scene."

I wait, holding my breath. That performance had felt good—really good—but with Professor Winters, you never know.

"It was..." he pauses, searching for the right word, "...promising."

Promising.

From Professor Winters, that was *everything!*

THREE

Varying Temperatures

DAVID HUNTER

THE HOLLOW CLICK of chalk against the blackboard echoes through the classroom as Professor Ramirez maps out a complex fluid dynamics equation. Most people would see gibberish. I see music—the formula for how water moves through a pipe system, how air flows over an aircraft wing.

"And this, gentlemen and ladies, is where most engineers make their fatal mistake." Ramirez circles a variable with dramatic flair. "They forget to account for viscosity at varying temperatures."

I've already jotted the correction in my notes, three lines ahead of where he's going. Engineering school isn't just my calling—it's where I finally make sense in the world.

Everyone here speaks my language. Numbers. Precision. Problems with actual solutions.

"Hunter," Ramirez points the chalk at me. "Solution?"

Without missing a beat, I answer, "You'd need to apply Reynolds transport theorem to account for the temperature differentials across the boundary layer."

Ramirez's mouth twitches into what passes for a smile from him. "Precisely. At least someone did the reading."

Jason, my lab partner, nudges me as Ramirez turns back to the board. "Show-off," he whispers.

I shrug. Can't help it if this stuff comes naturally.

When class ends, I'm surrounded before I can pack my laptop. Three classmates need help with the problem set. Two others want to confirm study group times. Another wants my notes from last week.

"David, you're still coming to Evan's party Friday, right?" Madison slides onto the desk in front of me, crossing her legs at an angle that's definitely calculated. Her red hair cascades over one shoulder as she leans forward.

"Wouldn't miss it," I flash the smile my sister Quinn calls my "lady-killer." The one that crinkles the corners of my eyes just enough.

"Good." Her fingers brush my arm. "I'll save you a dance."

"Or two," I counter, enjoying the blush that spreads across her cheeks.

I watch her walk away, knowing exactly what she's offering. Madison's been orbiting closer for weeks—smart, beautiful, and completely transparent about what she wants. Under different circumstances, I might be interested. But Madison is the relationship type. I've seen how she looks at me. Like I'm a puzzle she wants to solve. A wild thing she could tame.

Not happening.

Jason waits until she's out of earshot. "Dude, are you ever going to take her up on that?"

"On what?" I play dumb as we head out of the lecture hall.

"Don't even." Jason rolls his eyes. "Madison Calloway has been throwing herself at you all semester. She turned down Ryan Thompson—fucking Thompson—who's basically guaranteed a job at SpaceX after graduation."

I push through the double doors, sunlight hitting my face. "Not my type."

"Since when do you have a type? Besides 'female with a pulse'?"

The comment stings more than it should. My friends think they know me—the guy who charms his way through college, collecting phone numbers like trophies. They don't know about the nights I spend with my calculus proofs because they make more sense than people. They don't see me staring at my parents' wedding photo, wondering how two people could promise forever and end up such strangers.

"Maybe I'm evolving." I adjust my backpack.

"Into what? A monk?"

If he only knew.

I check my phone—a notification lights up the screen. A text from "N."

> Nikki: Same time tonight? Need to see you

My pulse jumps. Three simple lines of text shouldn't have this effect on me. I tap out a reply.

> David: My place 10pm. Ryder gone for the wkd

"Who's that got you smiling?" Jason tries to peek at my screen.

I lock the phone quickly. "Nobody."

"Bullshit. You've got a secret girlfriend."

"No girlfriend." That much is true. "Just plans."

Jason gives up as we reach the quad where our paths diverge. "Whatever, man. See you tomorrow for lab?"

"Yeah, I'll be there."

Alone finally, I cut through the engineering quad, nodding at familiar faces. Everyone knows everyone at Westlake Engineering Institute. It's exclusive, expensive, and exactly where I need to be to eventually design the next generation of impossible structures.

In my apartment off campus, I drop my backpack and immediately start straightening up. Not that Nikki complains about my organizational system—or lack thereof—but there's something about her that makes me want to impress her. Makes me want to be better than I am.

I change the sheets, pick up scattered clothes, and even wipe down the bathroom counter. All for a woman who won't even tell me her real name.

That's how we started this—fake names, no personal details, just chemistry so electric it should come with a warning label. She's Nikki. I'm Jax. We matched on Hinge three months ago, both looking for the same thing: something physical without complications. No strings, no histories, no expectations.

Just pleasure. Connection without commitment. The perfect arrangement.

I grab a beer from the fridge and sprawl on the couch, letting myself remember last Friday night. The way she looked showing up at my door in that tight black dress. How she kicked off her heels and climbed onto my lap without a word. The taste of whiskey on her lips. The sounds she made when I—

My phone buzzes again.

> Nikki: Running late. 10:30 ok?

I text back immediately.

> David: I'll wait up

I'd wait all night if I had to.

That thought stops me cold. When did this arrangement start feeling less casual? When did I start looking forward to her texts all day? When did I start wondering what her real name might be, what she studies, who she is when she's not in my bed?

Dangerous territory.

I take a long pull from my beer and remind myself of the rules. This works because we keep it simple. No complications. No real feelings. Just two adults using each other for release.

But my mind keeps circling back to her. The surprising intelligence behind her dark eyes. Her quick wit. The vulnerability that sometimes flashes across her face right after we finish, before she rebuilds her walls. The curve of her lips when she smiles against my chest in those rare moments she stays through the night.

Last week, she fell asleep here. I watched her breathing, watched how the streetlight through my blinds cast stripes across her brown skin. I traced the outline of her short curls against my pillow. I had the strangest urge to wake her up just to ask questions. Real questions. Who are you when you're not Nikki? What makes you laugh? What are you afraid of?

Instead, I let her sleep, went to my desk, and worked on problem sets until dawn, stealing glances at her between equations.

When she woke, she seemed disoriented, almost panicked to find herself still in my bed.

"This wasn't supposed to happen," she'd mumbled, gathering her clothes with uncharacteristic awkwardness.

"It's fine," I assured her. "Just sleep."

"Nothing is just sleep, Jax." The way she said my fake name felt like an accusation.

She'd left without her usual kiss goodbye, and I spent three days wondering if I'd broken something between us. Then last night, she texted again. Like nothing had changed.

I glance at the clock—8:47 pm. Almost two hours until she arrives. I should work on my fluid dynamics project. Should call my parents back. Should do anything except sit here counting minutes.

Instead, I find myself checking my phone again, rereading our sparse conversations. Looking for clues about who she really is, like some lovesick teenager.

This isn't me. I don't obsess over women. I don't count hours between seeing them. I definitely don't clean my apartment for them.

But Nikki isn't just any woman.

She's like a complicated equation I can't solve—all dark eyes and sharp edges and soft curves that fit perfectly against me. She's the only person who knows nothing about David Hunter—his family expectations, his academic reputation, his carefully constructed image—and still seems to see something in him worth coming back for.

I take another swig of beer, staring at the ceiling. I need to get my head straight before she gets here. Need to remember that this arrangement works because we keep it physical. Simple. Uncomplicated.

But lately, every time she leaves my bed, a strange emptiness follows. Every time she walks out my door, I fight the urge to ask her to stay. To have breakfast. To spend a day together that doesn't revolve around sex.

My phone buzzes with a campus alert—something about a water main break affecting the science building tomorrow. I dismiss it, disappointed it's not her.

This is getting pathetic. I force myself up, grab my laptop, and pull up my project files. I'll distract myself with work until 10:30. Focus on something productive instead of this strange, growing fixation.

But even as I stare at the screen, my mind betrays me—drifting to thoughts of her laugh, her scent, the way she looks at me when she thinks I don't notice.

Like I might be more than just a body to her too.

I pull up the Westlake Engineering design software on my laptop, but my mind refuses to focus on the pressure valve specifications. The cursor blinks accusingly as I stare at the screen, thoughts drifting back to her.

Nikki.

Even her fake name feels good in my mind. I've been with plenty of women—casual hookups, one-night stands, brief flings that burned hot and faded fast. But something about Nikki is different. Three months in, and she's still a mystery I can't unravel.

I close my laptop, accepting defeat. There's no point pretending I'll get any work done tonight.

What do I actually know about her? She's stunning—light brown skin that glows in the low light of my bedroom, curves that fit perfectly against my hands, short black curls that I love to run my fingers through when she allows it. She's smart—mentions books I've never heard of, catches references most people miss, challenges me in ways that go beyond physical.

But the real stuff? The details that make up a person? Nothing.

I don't know what she studies. Where she grew up. If she has siblings. What makes her laugh until she can't breathe. What keeps her up at night.

Should I ask her tonight?

The thought sends an uncomfortable ripple through my chest. Breaking our unspoken rules feels dangerous, like dismantling a perfectly calibrated machine just to see how it works.

No. Bad idea.

Our arrangement works precisely because we don't bring reality into it. No baggage, no expectations, no disappointment. Just two people who make each other feel good for a few stolen hours, then return to our separate lives until the next time.

I grab another beer from the fridge even though I shouldn't. Alcohol and curiosity make a dangerous combination, especially around her. Last time I had one too many, I almost asked about the small scar above her left eyebrow. Almost reached for my phone to suggest brunch the next morning.

Almost ruined everything.

I glance at the clock again. 9:38 pm. Still too much time to kill.

I can't sit still, so I pace around my apartment, straightening things that are already straight. The throw pillows on my couch—pillows I bought after the third time she came over, when she mentioned the place could use "softening up." The stack of engineering journals on my coffee table, arranged just so. The row of bottles on my kitchen counter—including the expensive whiskey she prefers.

When did I start building my life around her visits?

I catch my reflection in the bathroom mirror as I check my hair for the third time. I barely recognize myself—this guy anxiously waiting for a woman, planning his evening, his apartment, his drinks around her preferences.

"Get it together, Hunter," I mutter to my reflection.

I've never been this guy. David Hunter doesn't get attached. Doesn't get caught up. Doesn't rearrange his life for anyone. It's what keeps me safe—what I learned watching my parents' marriage dissolve into cold politeness and separate bedrooms.

People leave. Feelings fade. Better to keep things light than risk the inevitable crash.

But Nikki has me curious in ways no one else ever has.

What would happen if I broke the rules tonight? If I asked her real questions over that whiskey, before we fall into bed? If I suggested breakfast in the morning at that diner down the street?

No.

The word is firm in my mind. I can't risk it. What we have works. It's clean, uncomplicated. I get to be Jax with her—confident, carefree, unburdened by family expectations or academic pressure. She gets to be Nikki —whoever that is for her.

Reality would ruin it. Reality always does.

My phone vibrates on the counter. I lunge for it embarrassingly fast.

> Nikki: On my way. Need anything?

Such a simple text. Five words that shouldn't make my heart rate spike.

> David: Just you.

I stare at what I've typed, then quickly delete it. Too much. Too honest.

> David: All good. Door's unlocked.

I set my phone down and take a deep breath. I need to center myself before she gets here. Need to remember the parameters of what we're doing.

This isn't a relationship. It's an arrangement. I'd be an idiot to mess with a good thing just because I'm suddenly curious about the woman behind the fake name.

Still, as I hear the familiar sound of her car pulling into my apartment complex's lot, something tightens in my chest. An anticipation that goes beyond the physical.

I move to the window, watching her step out of her car —a small dark blue Honda that's seen better days. She looks up at my window as if she can sense me watching, and for a second, our eyes meet across the parking lot. She gives a small wave, adjusting the strap of her bag on her shoulder.

Even from this distance, even through the darkness, something about her steals my breath. The confident way she moves. The curve of her silhouette under the streetlight.

I step back from the window, suddenly feeling like a stalker. Get it together, Hunter.

I listen to her footsteps coming up the stairs to my second-floor apartment, each one making my pulse quicken. The soft knock that follows is just a courtesy—she knows the door is unlocked for her.

"It's open," I call, trying to sound casual, like I haven't been counting minutes.

And then she's there, stepping into my apartment, closing the door behind her. Tonight, she's wearing simple black leggings and an oversized sweater that slips off one shoulder. Her makeup is minimal, her hair in its natural curls. She looks tired but still stunning.

"Hey," she says, dropping her bag by the door.

"Hey yourself," I respond, leaning against the kitchen counter, trying to look relaxed. "Rough day?"

She sighs, kicking off her shoes. "The roughest. I need…" She trails off, looking at me with those deep brown eyes that see too much.

"What do you need?" I ask, my voice dropping lower.

"You," she answers simply, closing the distance between us in three steps. "Just you."

Her hands find my face, and then she's kissing me like she's drowning and I'm oxygen. I respond immediately, pulling her against me, my fingers sliding beneath that oversized sweater to find warm skin.

This—this I understand. This is our language, the one we speak fluently together. My curiosity about her life fades beneath the more urgent need to rediscover her body.

I lift her onto the counter, standing between her legs as she wraps them around my waist. She tastes like mint gum and something sweeter—maybe the fruity cocktail I can smell faintly on her breath.

"Did you start without me?" I murmur against her jaw, trailing kisses down her neck.

She laughs, the sound vibrating against my lips. "Just one drink with a friend. Needed liquid courage."

"For me? I'm hurt, Nikki." I pull back to look at her, grinning. "After all this time, you still need courage?"

Something flickers in her eyes—a shadow I can't quite read. "Not for this part," she says, rolling her hips against mine. "Never for this part."

I want to ask what she means. Want to push past the boundaries we've set. But then she's tugging at my t-shirt, and my questions dissolve into more immediate concerns.

We don't make it to the bedroom the first time. The counter, then the couch—urgent and heated, like we're trying to exorcise something from our systems. It's always like this with her—desperate at first, like we can't get close enough, can't get deep enough.

Later, in my bed, it's different. Slower. I take my time mapping her body with my hands, my lips. Memorizing her reactions, the small sounds she makes when I touch her just right. The way her back arches when she's close. The flutter of her eyelashes against her cheeks.

Nikki has me completely captivated. She's the best sex I've ever had—not just because she's gorgeous or because she knows what she's doing. It's because she's fully present in these moments. There's an honesty in the way she responds to me, a vulnerability she allows herself here that I suspect she rarely shows elsewhere.

After, as we lie tangled in my sheets, her head on my chest, I find myself tracing patterns on her bare shoulder. The questions I swore not to ask hover on the tip of my tongue.

Who are you, really? What's your real name? What are you studying? Do you think about me when we're apart?

But I don't ask any of them. I let the comfortable silence stretch between us, feeling her heartbeat gradually slow against mine.

"What are you thinking?" she murmurs, her fingers making lazy circles on my stomach.

I hesitate. "That you're amazing," I say finally, keeping it simple. Safe.

She lifts her head to look at me, her expression unreadable. For a moment, I think she's going to push—going to ask the real question behind her question.

Instead, she smiles, a soft, almost sad curve of her lips. "You're not so bad yourself, Jax."

FOUR

Random Moments

WHITNEY BARNES

THE DIGITAL CLOCK on Jax's nightstand blinks 2:17 AM, its red glow the only light in his bedroom besides the silver moonlight filtering through half-closed blinds. I'm sprawled across his sheets, my body still humming from our second round. The cotton beneath me is damp with sweat—ours mingled together in the most primal way.

"Damn," I whisper, staring up at the ceiling fan making lazy circles above us. My breath hasn't fully returned yet. "That was..."

"Fucking incredible?" Jax finishes my sentence, his voice a satisfied rumble beside me.

I turn my head to look at him. In this light, his blonde hair appears almost silver, and those hazel eyes catch every bit of available light like they're designed to glow in the dark. His chest rises and falls with deep breaths, a thin sheen of sweat making his skin gleam. There's something about seeing him like this—completely undone, walls down—that makes me want to know more.

Which is dangerous. That's not what we do.

I trace a finger along his bicep, following a vein down to his wrist. "Can I ask you something?"

He shifts slightly, muscles tensing under my touch. "Depends what it is, Nikki."

The fake name still sounds natural coming from him, even though it feels increasingly strange on my end. We've been hooking up for almost three months now. I've memorized every inch of his body, know exactly how to make him groan my name—my fake name—but I don't know the first real thing about him.

"What do you do? Like, for work or school or whatever." The question hangs between us, violating our unspoken agreement to keep things strictly physical.

Jax's body stiffens further. His jaw tightens, Adam's apple bobbing as he swallows. For a second, I think he might tell me to leave.

"Marketing," he finally says, eyes fixed on the ceiling. "I'm studying marketing."

"Really?" I prop myself up on one elbow, suddenly interested. "What kind?"

He hesitates, then shrugs with calculated casualness. "Marketing Research Analyst, market trends and shit. Nothing exciting."

Something about his answer feels off. Not necessarily a lie, but not the complete truth either. He's sharing the minimum to satisfy my curiosity.

"That's cool. What made you choose that?" I push, knowing I'm crossing our carefully drawn boundaries but unable to stop myself.

His eyes flick to mine, a flash of warning in them. "My old man." He smirks, but it doesn't reach his eyes. "Anyway, what about you? What's your deal when you're not in my bed?"

The deflection is so smooth I almost miss it, but now I'm on the receiving end of the uncomfortable questioning. Fair is fair.

"I'm in school too," I say, which isn't a lie. I consider telling him about my drama major, my auditions, my dreams—but something stops me. These details feel too personal, too real. Once we start exchanging truths, where does it end?

"Studying business," I lie, the words tasting wrong on my tongue. "My mom's idea. She wants me to take over the family company someday."

"Family company?" His eyebrow raises in interest.

"Real estate," I elaborate, building on the fiction. "Nothing as fancy as it sounds. Just a small firm in Connecticut." I've never even been to Connecticut.

Jax studies me for a long moment, his eyes narrowed slightly. "Huh. Wouldn't have pegged you for a future CEO."

"No?" I try to keep my voice light. "What would you have pegged me for?"

"Something more... creative." His gaze sweeps over my face, lingering on my lips. "You've got that artistic vibe."

My heart skips. Does he see through my lie? Or is he just exceptionally perceptive? Either way, I need to change the subject before he digs deeper.

"My turn for a question," I say, tracing patterns on his chest. "Have you always lived in—"

His mouth captures mine mid-sentence. His hand slides up to cup my face, thumb stroking my cheek as his tongue teases my lower lip. The distraction technique is obvious but effective. My body responds instantly, arching toward him even as my mind registers what he's doing.

"No more questions," he murmurs against my lips. "I can think of better ways to use this mouth."

His hand slides down my neck, palm flat against my collarbone. I should call him out, push back against this blatant deflection. But his touch leaves fire in its wake, and my resistance melts with each passing second.

"You're changing the subject," I manage to say, though it comes out breathier than intended.

"Damn right I am." He grins against my skin, trailing kisses down my throat. "You complaining?"

I'm not. That's the problem. Jax knows exactly how to short-circuit my brain, how to make me forget everything except the feel of his hands on my body.

His mouth continues its journey downward, passing between my breasts, lingering to taste the sweat in the valley between them. My fingers find his hair, threading through the soft strands as heat pools low in my belly.

This is familiar territory—safe territory. Bodies speaking a language that requires no names, no histories, no complications.

"God, you're beautiful," he whispers against my stomach, his breath hot on my skin. "Every fucking inch of you."

His hands grip my thighs, spreading them wider as he settles between them. The first touch of his tongue makes me gasp, back arching off the bed. He knows exactly how to touch me, alternating between soft, teasing laps and firm pressure that makes my toes curl. Three months of learning each other's bodies has made him dangerously skilled at unraveling me.

My mind empties of everything except sensation—the wet heat of his mouth, the slight scratch of stubble against my inner thighs, the tightening coil of pleasure building at my core. Questions about his life, my lies, all of it fades to white noise beneath the symphony he's playing on my body.

"Jax," I moan, hips rising to meet his mouth. "God, yes. Right there."

He groans against me, the vibration sending shockwaves through my system. His hands slide beneath me, gripping my ass to lift me higher, giving him better access. I'm completely at his mercy, and we both know it.

When I'm right at the edge, trembling and desperate, he pulls away. I make a sound of protest that turns into a gasp as he crawls up my body, positioning himself at my entrance.

"Look at me," he commands, and I obey, meeting those hazel eyes now dark with desire.

He enters me in one smooth thrust, filling me completely. We both groan at the sensation. There's no tenderness here, no gentle lovemaking—just raw, primal need. His hips snap against mine, setting a punishing pace that has me clawing at his back, leaving half-moon indentations with my nails.

"Fuck, Nikki," he pants, his forehead pressed against mine. "You feel so good. So fucking tight."

His words are filthy and perfect, pushing me closer to the edge. I wrap my legs around his waist, changing the angle, taking him even deeper. The new position hits exactly where I need it, and I feel myself clenching around him.

"I'm close," I gasp, digging my heels into his lower back.

"Come for me," he growls, one hand sliding between our bodies to circle my clit. "Now."

The combined stimulation sends me flying over the edge, my orgasm crashing through me in intense waves. I cry out his name—his fake name—as my body convulses around him. He follows seconds later, his rhythm faltering as he buries himself deep, his release hot inside me.

For a few moments, we stay connected, both breathing heavily. His weight presses me into the mattress, but I don't mind. There's something comforting about being completely covered by him, sheltered from the world for just a little longer.

Eventually, he rolls off me, flopping onto his back beside me. Neither of us speaks right away. The questions from earlier hang in the air between us, but the urgency has dissipated, at least temporarily.

"Water?" he asks finally, sitting up.

"Please."

He pads naked to the kitchen, giving me a perfect view of his sculpted back, the dimples just above his ass, the powerful thighs that were between mine moments ago. I allow myself to appreciate the view, pushing away the nagging thought that I want to know more about the man inside that perfect body.

I watch Jax's naked form disappear around the corner, the muscles in his back shifting under tan skin as he moves. My body still tingles from his touch, but my mind has already started its familiar spiral.

What am I doing?

This question haunts me more with each passing hookup. At first, this arrangement was perfect—hot, no-strings sex with a gorgeous guy who doesn't even know my real name. No expectations, no disappointments, no vulnerability. Just pleasure in its purest form.

But something's changing.

I roll onto my side, pulling the sheet up to cover myself even though he's seen every inch of me countless times. The bed smells like him—like us—a musky cocktail of sweat, sex, and that woodsy cologne he always wears. I breathe it in, closing my eyes.

Three months of this. Three months of sneaking to his apartment under the cover of darkness, three months of lying to Quinn about where I'm going, three months of creating increasingly elaborate stories about "study groups" and "late rehearsals." All to maintain this carefully constructed fantasy where we're just bodies satisfying a mutual need.

But fantasies have expiration dates, don't they?

I hear the tap running in the kitchen, the clink of glasses. Such a mundane, domestic sound in the middle of our deliberately non-domestic arrangement.

Would he want to date me out in the sunlight? Like a legit couple?

The thought makes my stomach flip in a way that has nothing to do with the orgasms he just gave me. I try to picture it—holding hands with him in public, introducing him to friends, taking actual dates instead of booty calls. Would he open doors for me? Would he get jealous if other guys looked my way? Would he sit through one of my performances and bring me flowers afterward?

The image is so tempting it hurts.

But then reality crashes in. We don't even know each other's real names. This relationship—if you can call it that—was built on a foundation of lies from day one. By mutual agreement, sure, but lies nonetheless. How do you transition from fake identities and forbidden questions to actual dating?

"Here you go."

His voice startles me from my thoughts. He's standing by the bed, extending a glass of water toward me. The moonlight catches on the droplets running down the side, making them sparkle like tiny diamonds.

"Thanks," I say, sitting up and taking the glass, careful to keep the sheet covering my breasts. It's ridiculous to suddenly feel modest after what we just did, but something about this moment feels different. More vulnerable.

He sits on the edge of the bed, facing away from me as he drinks his water. The silence between us feels charged now, like the air before a thunderstorm.

Does he have feelings for me?

I study the curve of his spine, the way his hair curls slightly at the nape of his neck where it's growing too long. I know his body intimately—every scar, every sensitive spot, exactly how to touch him to make him come undone. But I know nothing about what goes on inside his head when we're not together.

Does he think about me during the day? Does he ever start to type my name—my fake name—into his phone, then delete it because we're not supposed to communicate outside our hookups? Does he ever wish for more than this physical connection we've established?

I take another sip of water, searching for courage in the mundane act of hydration.

"Jax," I begin, my voice smaller than I intended.

He turns his head slightly, profile illuminated by moonlight. "Yeah?"

The words stick in my throat. What exactly am I planning to say? 'Hey, I know we agreed this was just casual sex, but I might be developing feelings for you even though I don't actually know who you are'? How pathetic would that sound?

"Nothing," I mutter, looking down at my glass. "Just... thanks for the water."

He laughs softly, the sound containing a hint of relief that makes my chest tighten. "You're welcome. Very polite for someone who was screaming obscenities a few minutes ago."

I force a smile, but my mind has latched onto a new, terrible thought.

Just then, the weirdest thought entered my head - does he sleep with other girls besides me? Exclusivity was never discussed - *did he?*

The image flashes unbidden—Jax's hands on another woman's body, his mouth trailing down her throat, his hips moving between her thighs. A wave of nausea rolls through me, sudden and visceral.

Of course he does. Why wouldn't he? We never promised each other anything. For all I know, he has a different girl in this bed every night of the week. Maybe I'm Monday. Maybe there's a Tuesday waiting for his text right now.

The water in my glass suddenly tastes bitter. I set it on the nightstand, my appetite for everything gone.

"You okay?" He's looking at me now, eyebrows drawn together in confusion.

"Fine," I lie, avoiding his gaze. "Just tired."

"Tired?" He scoots closer, one hand coming to rest on my sheet-covered thigh. "That's a first. Usually you're ready for round three by now."

His touch, which normally sends electricity through me, now feels like it's burning my skin through the fabric. I shift away slightly, and his hand falls back to the bed.

The confusion in his eyes deepens.

"It's late," I say, glancing at the clock. "I have an early... business class tomorrow."

Another lie to add to our collection. I don't have class until noon tomorrow.

He studies me for a long moment, like he's trying to read something written in a language he doesn't understand. "If you say so."

I should ask. I should just open my mouth and ask if he's sleeping with other women. It's a reasonable question, even in a casual arrangement. Sexual health and all that. But the words won't come.

I'm too scared of the answer.

Because what if he says yes? What if he casually confirms that I'm just one of many, a body to satisfy his needs when the mood strikes? What if he looks confused that I would even ask, reminding me that we agreed this was just physical from the beginning?

Or worse—what if he turns the question back on me? Am I sleeping with other men?

The answer is no. There's been no one else since I met him. Not for lack of opportunities—Quinn's tried to set me up with guys from her classes, and I've had plenty of offers at campus parties. But every time, I find myself making excuses, claiming to be focused on my studies or my acting.

The truth is, no one else measures up to Jax. No one else makes me feel the way he does—not just physically, but the way my heart races when I see his name on my phone, the way I catch myself smiling at random moments remembering something he said.

God, I'm in deeper than I thought.

"I should go," I say abruptly, gathering the sheet around me as I stand.

Jax's eyes follow me as I move around the room, collecting my scattered clothes. "You're not staying?" There's genuine surprise in his voice. I've spent the night almost every time in the last month.

"Can't." The word comes out clipped. "Like I said, early morning."

I dress with my back to him, suddenly self-conscious. The silence in the room is deafening. When I'm fully clothed, I finally turn to face him.

He's still sitting on the bed, sheet pooled around his

waist, watching me with an expression I can't quite read. Confusion? Annoyance? Hurt? Maybe all three.

"Is something wrong?" he asks eventually. "You seem... off."

I force a casual shrug. "Nothing's wrong. Just tired and busy."

He doesn't believe me. I can see it in his eyes. But he doesn't push, because pushing would violate our unspoken rules. No deep questions, no emotional complications.

"Okay." He runs a hand through his hair, making it stand up in messy spikes. "When will I see you again?"

The question sends a fresh wave of anxiety through me. Part of me wants to say "never"—to cut this off before I fall any deeper into whatever this is. Another part wants to crawl back into bed with him and never leave.

"I'll text you," I say, which commits me to nothing.

He nods slowly. "Right."

I grab my purse, checking for my keys and phone. Everything in order for my escape. "So... bye."

"See ya."

I get outta there as fast as I can.

FIVE

A Leather Wallet

DAVID HUNTER

I PULL into the driveway of my childhood home, cutting the engine of my Camaro and sitting for a moment. The two-story colonial looks exactly like it has for the past twenty-two years of my life—pristine white trim, navy shutters, perfectly manicured lawn. Mom's Volvo sits in its usual spot. Dad's Mercedes is gone, as expected.

Just a random Wednesday afternoon visit. No reason. At least that's what I tell myself as I grab the bag of muffins I picked up from her favorite bakery downtown.

The front door opens before I even reach it.

"David!" Mom's face lights up like I've been gone for years instead of three weeks. Her blonde hair—where I got mine—is pulled back in a neat ponytail, and she's wearing one of those fancy athleisure outfits that probably cost more than my textbooks.

"Hey, Mom." I lean down to hug her, breathing in the familiar scent of her Chanel perfume.

"This is such a wonderful surprise!" She pulls back, examining my face like she's checking for evidence of something. "Why didn't you tell me you were coming? I would've made your favorite lasagna."

I hold up the bakery bag. "Brought muffins. Thought maybe we could have lunch."

Her smile widens. "Perfect timing. I just finished my Pilates session and was about to make something."

I follow her into the kitchen—all stainless steel and marble, practically untouched despite being renovated three years ago. Dad insisted on top-of-the-line everything, but he's barely home to enjoy any of it.

"Coffee?" Mom asks, already reaching for the fancy machine that requires an engineering degree to operate.

"Sure." I hop onto one of the barstools at the counter, watching her move around the kitchen with practiced efficiency.

"So," she says, her back to me as she prepares our drinks, "how's school? Still acing everything?"

"Pretty much." I shrug, though she can't see it. "Professor Keller wants me to consider the research program for next summer."

"That's wonderful!" She turns, beaming with that specific type of pride that used to embarrass me as a teenager but now feels... nice. "Your father will be thrilled."

"Where is he, anyway?" I ask, though I already know.

"Conference in Chicago. Back Friday." She slides a perfect cappuccino in front of me, complete with a leaf design in the foam. "Now, what would you like for lunch? I have ingredients for sandwiches, or I could whip up some—"

"Sandwiches are fine." I take a sip of coffee. "Let me help."

We work side by side, assembling turkey and avocado on sourdough. It feels comfortable, this routine. Mom chatters about neighborhood gossip and her latest charity committee, and I nod at the appropriate moments.

But something feels off. Has it always been there? This underlying tension in her voice when she mentions Dad? The way her eyes don't quite match her smile?

We settle at the kitchen table with our sandwiches and coffee, sunlight streaming through the windows that overlook the backyard.

"So," I say after a few minutes of small talk, "are you happy, Mom?"

The question hangs between us. Her sandwich stops halfway to her mouth.

"What do you mean?" She puts it down, carefully aligning it with the edge of her plate.

"Just... are you happy? With your life, with..." I gesture vaguely around us, at this perfect house that sometimes feels more like a museum than a home.

She reaches for her water, taking a small sip. Her wedding ring catches the light—three carats, platinum band, recently cleaned.

"That's quite a question for lunch on a Wednesday." Her laugh doesn't reach her eyes.

"Just wondering." I take another bite, giving her space to ignore it if she wants.

She traces the rim of her coffee cup with one manicured finger. "Why do you ask?"

I shrug. "Engineering school. We're trained to observe patterns, analyze data."

"And what pattern are you seeing?" Her tone is light, but her knuckles whiten around her cup.

"You don't talk about Dad the way you used to."

The silence stretches between us, charged with all the things we've never said out loud.

"No." The word is so quiet I almost miss it. "No, I'm not happy." She looks up, meeting my eyes directly. "Not in the way you're asking."

My chest tightens. It's one thing to suspect—another to hear it confirmed.

"What happened?" I ask.

She sighs, releasing years of held breath. "Nothing dramatic. That's almost the saddest part. We just... drifted. Your father works. I organize. We live separate lives under the same roof."

"How long?"

"Years." She gives me a small, sad smile. "Probably since you left for college. Maybe before. It's hard to pinpoint when love starts to fade."

"Then why stay?" The question comes out harsher than I intended.

She doesn't flinch. "Financial stability. Security. Habit." She gestures around the kitchen. "Your father is a good provider. Always has been."

"But isn't being happy more important than—"

"It's complicated, David." Her voice firms. "Marriage is complicated. You make compromises. You make choices."

"Compromising your happiness seems like a pretty big sacrifice." I push the remains of my sandwich away, my appetite gone.

"When you've been with someone for twenty-five years, the equation changes." She reaches across the table, covering my hand with hers. "And there are different kinds of happiness. I have my friends, my charity work. I have you and your sister."

"But you deserve—"

"What I deserve and what's practical aren't always the same thing." She squeezes my hand. "That's part of being an adult."

The thought hits me like a sucker punch to the gut. Is this what relationships inevitably become? A slow slide from passion to pragmatism, from love to logistics?

"I never want to get married." The declaration bursts out of me. "Ever."

Mom tilts her head, studying me. "That's a pretty definitive statement for someone your age."

"I mean it. What's the point? So I can end up—" I stop myself, but it's too late.

"Like me and your father?" She finishes, her voice gentle.

"I didn't mean—"

"It's okay." She withdraws her hand, collecting our plates. "Not all marriages end up like ours. Look at the Hendersons next door—thirty years and still holding hands on their evening walks."

I follow her to the sink, taking the dishes from her to load into the dishwasher. "Seems like the exception, not the rule."

"Maybe." She leans against the counter. "But closing yourself off to possibilities isn't the answer either." Her eyes narrow slightly. "Is there someone special making you think about this? Someone you're seeing?"

Nikki's face flashes in my mind—her dark eyes, the way she throws her head back when she laughs, how her skin feels against mine in the darkness of my apartment. The way my chest tightens when she texts, how I find myself checking my phone more often, hoping to see her name.

"No," I say firmly, shutting down that dangerous line of thinking. "Focusing on school right now."

Mom raises an eyebrow. "That flush on your cheeks says otherwise."

"It's hot in here." I turn away, adjusting the dishwasher racks with unnecessary force.

"David." Her voice has that mom-knows-better tone. "You don't have to tell me about her. But don't let what's happening between your father and me color your view of relationships."

"It's nothing serious," I insist, more to myself than to her. "Just... casual."

But is it? Every time Nikki leaves my apartment, it gets harder to watch her go. Every time she shares a small detail about herself—breaking our unspoken rules—I store it away like something precious. Why does my chest ache when I think about her with someone else? Why do I find myself wanting to tell her things I've never told anyone?

"Just be careful," Mom says, misinterpreting my silence. "Casual has a way of becoming complicated when hearts get involved."

"My heart's not involved," I say automatically. The lie tastes bitter.

Mom gives me a knowing look but doesn't push it. "So, tell me more about this research program Professor Keller mentioned."

I latch onto the subject change gratefully, launching into details about computational engineering and summer stipends. But part of my mind stays fixed on Nikki—on the growing feeling that what we have is shifting into something I never planned for, something that terrifies me more than any equation or problem set ever could.

Why can't I stop thinking about her? Why do I keep wanting more?

I excuse myself, mumbling something about wanting to see if my old PlayStation games are still in my room. Mom gives me that look—the one that says she knows there's more going on than I'm letting on, but she'll let me have my space.

"Your room's exactly as you left it," she calls after me. "I dust once a week but otherwise haven't touched a thing."

The stairs creak in all the familiar places. Three steps from the top—that loud one I always skipped when sneaking in after curfew. The upstairs hallway is lined with family photos, a visual timeline of the Hunter family. Dad in his golf attire. My sister, in her graduation cap. Me, holding various sports trophies, grinning like I'd just discovered the secret to happiness.

Funny how none of those smiles feel familiar anymore.

I push open my bedroom door. The hinges whine softly, protesting after weeks of disuse. The smell hits me immediately—a mix of old cologne, laundry detergent, and something distinctly... mine. Like my DNA has permanently marked this space.

"Jesus," I whisper, scanning the room.

A Leather Wallet

Mom wasn't kidding. It's a perfect time capsule of eighteen-year-old me. Navy blue bedspread perfectly tucked in (her doing, not mine). Engineering posters on the walls next to football pennants. The contradiction that was—still is—my existence.

I sit on the edge of the bed, half expecting it to give way under my weight. When did I get too big for this space? The mattress dips, familiar and strange all at once. My eyes drift to the bookshelf where trophies line the top shelf—football, basketball, track. The golden figures frozen mid-action, celebrating victories that seemed so important at the time.

"Just a jock," I mutter, reaching up to tap the football player's helmet. The metal is cool against my finger. "That's all anyone saw."

But not all. The bottom shelves tell a different story—science fair medals, academic decathlon ribbons, dog-eared textbooks I couldn't bear to part with. The duality of David Hunter: athlete and brain, never fully one or the other.

I lean back on my hands, letting the quiet of the room settle around me. From downstairs, I can faintly hear Mom on the phone—probably calling Dad to tell him I stopped by. Their routine dance of polite updates and separate lives.

Is that what relationships are? Two people moving around each other in carefully choreographed patterns until the music stops and you realize you've been dancing alone the entire time?

My gaze drifts to the dresser. Three drawers of clothes I outgrew years ago. But the top drawer—that was always my secret space. Where eighteen-year-old me kept everything that mattered.

I cross the room in two strides, pulling open the drawer. The smell of cedar and forgotten cologne wafts up. Neatly folded socks and underwear, arranged in perfect rows—again, Mom's doing. I reach beneath the back corner, feeling for the leather edge I know is there.

My fingers close around it, and something in my chest clenches.

The wallet is cracked and worn, the leather softened from years of being carried in my back pocket throughout high school. I haven't seen it since the day I left for college, when I deliberately tucked it away and bought a new one. Clean slate. New life.

A Leather Wallet

I open it slowly. A few faded dollar bills. An ancient GameStop gift card. My first driver's license with that terrible haircut I thought looked cool. And behind the plastic photo sleeve, where most guys kept condoms, there she is.

Melanie Jackson.

The 4x6 photo is slightly bent at the corners, but her smile is as bright as ever. Another black beauty—I've always been attracted to black girls. Long, dark, straight hair falling in waves past her shoulders. That tiny mole above her right eyebrow that I used to kiss. Her arms wrapped around my waist at the beach, senior year spring break. Both of us sun-kissed and laughing, unaware that three months later she'd rip my heart out and stomp on it with her Converse high-tops.

"Fuck," I whisper, running my thumb over her face.

It's been four years, but the memory still stings. The girl I gave everything to—my first real girlfriend, first person I trusted with all my secrets, first time I let someone see past the jock facade. First "I love you" that actually meant something.

The same girl who told me, two weeks before we were supposed to leave for separate colleges, that she'd been sleeping with my best friend for months.

"It just happened, David. We didn't mean to hurt you. But Asher and I... there's something real between us. More real than what you and I had."

More real. Like three years together had been some kind of practice run. Like I'd been a placeholder until something better came along.

I snap the wallet shut, the sound sharp in the quiet room. My chest feels tight, like someone's wrapping piano wire around my ribs and slowly, methodically, tightening it.

This is why. This right here—this feeling like I'm eighteen again, standing in my driveway watching Melanie drive away for the last time. This hollow ache that didn't fully heal for over a year.

This is why I don't do relationships. Why I keep things casual. Why "Jax" exists—to keep people at arm's length where they can't reach the parts of me that matter. Where they can't touch the soft, vulnerable spots still tender from the last time I let someone in.

And Nikki... *fuck*. Nikki is *dangerous*.

Because when she asks me personal questions in the darkness of my apartment, part of me wants to answer. When she traces patterns on my skin after we've had sex, I find myself wanting to tell her stories about these scars. When she falls asleep against my chest, I catch myself watching her, memorizing the curve of her cheek and the flutter of her eyelashes.

I'm breaking all my own rules with her.

Just last night, lying in bed after round two, she turned to me with those big dark eyes.

"What made you become a marketing major?" she asked, voice soft in the dim light.

Our agreement has always been simple: no personal questions, no real names, no backstories. Just two bodies finding pleasure together, then going our separate ways until the next time. Clean. Simple. Safe.

I should have deflected. Should have kissed her to silence—or made a joke.

Instead, I found myself telling her about the summer I broke my arm in football practice and spent weeks building elaborate Rube Goldberg machines in my bedroom to pass the time. How I realized I loved the precision of it, the problem-solving, the way all the pieces had to work perfectly together.

She smiled at me like I'd given her a gift. And it felt good—too good—to share that piece of myself with her.

Dangerous territory.

I tuck the wallet back under the socks, exactly where eighteen-year-old me left it. A reminder of what happens when you let people too close. When you give them the map of all your weak spots and secret places.

Standing up, I take one last look around the room. At the trophies and medals, the posters and pennants. The remnants of a version of myself that believed in love and forever and happily-ever-afters. Before I learned that love is just another word for vulnerability, and vulnerability is just another word for pain.

This is why Nikki can't be more than she is—a warm body in my bed, a temporary escape, a mutual arrangement between consenting adults.

Because if I let her be more, if I let myself feel more, I'll end up right back here—sitting in a room full of memories, nursing wounds that never quite heal right.

I head back downstairs, stepping over that creaky third step from the top. Mom's in the kitchen, wiping down already-clean counters. Her own form of therapy.

"Find what you were looking for?" she asks, not looking up.

I think about the wallet, about Melanie's smile, about the way Nikki looked last night when she slipped out of my apartment.

"Yeah," I say, forcing a smile. "Found exactly what I needed to remember."

SIX

Channeling

WHITNEY BARNES

MY HEAD SPINS with the swirling emotions of Lady Macbeth as I pace across the dusty stage of our university's black box theater. The harsh spotlight catches every movement, casting dramatic shadows that stretch like fingers across the worn floorboards. Professor Winters sits in the third row, her silver-rimmed glasses perched on her nose, scrutinizing my every gesture.

"Again, Whitney. From 'Out, damned spot,'" she calls, her voice echoing through the empty seats.

I close my eyes, centering myself, channeling the madness of a woman consumed by guilt. When I open them, I'm no longer Whitney Barnes—I'm a Scottish queen unraveling at the seams.

"Out, damned spot! Out, I say!" My voice cracks with desperation as I frantically rub at my hands. "One, two—why then, 'tis time to do't. Hell is murky—"

The sudden vibration in my pocket breaks my concentration. I stumble over the next line, my character slipping away like water through fingers.

"Sorry," I mutter, stepping out of character. "My phone—"

Professor Winters sighs, making no attempt to hide her disappointment. "Take five, everyone. Whitney, please remember that your devices should be silenced during rehearsal."

Heat rushes to my cheeks as I fumble for my phone. My mother's name flashes across the screen, and I hesitate before answering. It's unusual for her to call during my scheduled rehearsal time.

"I need to take this," I tell Professor Winters, already backing toward the wings.

Once in the dimly lit backstage area, surrounded by hanging costumes and prop tables, I answer. "Mom? What's going on?"

"Whitney, honey." Her voice has that specific tone—the one that means she's about to disappoint me. "I'm calling to let you know I've been assigned a last-minute business trip to Seattle. I'll be gone through the Thanksgiving holiday."

The words hit me like a physical blow. "Wait, what? You're not going to be home for Thanksgiving?"

"I'm sorry, sweetheart. The company needs me to close this deal, and—"

"It's Thanksgiving, Mom." My voice drops to a harsh whisper. "Our holiday. The one time of year we actually sit down together."

"I know, and I feel terrible about it. Maybe you could join me in Seattle? The company would cover your flight."

I laugh, the sound hollow and brittle. "I have rehearsals until Tuesday night. The showcase is right after break."

"Well, then..." She trails off, and I can picture her perfectly—standing in her immaculate kitchen, designer glasses pushed up into her hair, calendar app open on her tablet. Always organized, always planning. Always putting her career first.

"It's fine," I say, even though it's not. "I'll figure something out."

"I'll make it up to you at Christmas. I promise."

Promises. She's good at those. Following through? Not so much.

"I have to go," I tell her. "I'm in the middle of rehearsal."

"I love you, Whitney."

I end the call without responding, staring at the dark screen. Thanksgiving. Suddenly the realization crashes over me—the break starts in three days. Between rehearsals, assignments, and late-night texts with Jax, I've completely lost track of time.

What am I supposed to do *now*? Spend the holiday alone in a nearly empty dorm, eating microwave ramen while my mother wines and dines potential clients?

My phone buzzes with a text.

> Jax: Tonight?

Even that—the one thing that usually makes my pulse quicken—falls flat. I shove my phone back into my pocket without responding.

When I return to the stage, Professor Winters is giving notes to the other actors. She looks up as I approach, and something in my expression makes her pause.

"Everything all right, Whitney?"

I force a smile. "Fine."

But she's been teaching drama for twenty years. She sees through the performance.

"Everyone take ten," she announces to the group. As the other students scatter, she motions for me to sit beside her in the front row.

"What's going on?" she asks once we're alone.

I shrug, picking at a loose thread on my jeans. "Just family stuff. Nothing important."

"Doesn't look like nothing."

The theater's silence wraps around us, strangely comforting. Dust motes dance in the beam of the ghost light.

"My mom just called to tell me she's bailing on Thanksgiving. Business trip." I try to keep my voice neutral, but the hurt and anger seep through anyway.

Professor Winters nods slowly. "That's disappointing."

"Yeah, well. Not the first time."

"You know," she says, looking toward the empty stage, "what I just witnessed when you came back—that raw emotion, that authentic hurt and anger—that's *exactly* what I've been trying to pull out of you for Lady Macbeth."

I follow her gaze. "What do you mean?"

"Your best performances will always come from tapping into real feelings. Not manufactured ones." She turns back to me, her eyes intense. "Don't waste those emotions, Whitney. Use them. Channel them. Let Lady Macbeth's guilt and desperation become a vehicle for your own frustrations."

The idea clicks into place, making perfect sense. "Method acting."

"In a way, yes. Though I prefer to think of it as emotional honesty. The audience can always tell the difference between performed emotions and real ones."

When we resume rehearsal, I find myself sinking deeper into Lady Macbeth's madness than ever before, letting my own anger and disappointment fuel her descent. The words flow naturally, urgently. When I finish the scene, the theater is completely silent.

Professor Winters removes her glasses. "That," she says simply, "is what we've been working toward."

The validation should feel good, but by the time I trudge back to my dorm room that evening, I'm emotionally drained. The anger has cooled into a dull ache of disappointment. My mother has always put her career first, but holidays were supposed to be our sacred time. The one tradition we maintained after my father left.

I unlock our door to find Quinn sprawled across her bed, textbook open but clearly forgotten as she scrolls through her phone. She looks up when I enter, her blonde hair twisted into a messy bun on top of her head.

"You look like hell warmed over," she observes cheerfully.

I dump my backpack on the floor and collapse face-first onto my bed. "Thanks. That's exactly what every girl wants to hear."

"Rough rehearsal?"

I roll onto my back, staring at the water stain on our ceiling. "Rough everything. My mom just informed me she's skipping town for Thanksgiving. Some emergency business trip."

Quinn sits up, frowning. "Seriously? That sucks."

"Yeah. And I totally forgot break was coming up until

she called. Now I'm scrambling to figure out what to do."

"Wait, you're not planning to stay here, are you?" Quinn looks genuinely horrified at the thought.

I shrug. "Not many options. The dining hall will be closed, but I've got cup noodles and desperation."

"Absolutely not." Quinn tosses her phone aside and swings her legs off the bed. "You're coming home with me for Thanksgiving."

"Quinn, I can't just invite myself to your family's—"

"You're not inviting yourself. I'm inviting you." She fixes me with her no-nonsense stare. "My mom goes full Martha Stewart for Thanksgiving. She makes three different kinds of pie, her own cranberry sauce—not that canned garbage—and stuffing that will make you want to slap somebody."

Despite myself, I smile. "Sounds intense."

"It is. We're talking place cards, cloth napkins, the whole nine yards. She'd be thrilled to have another person at the table. Especially someone who appreciates good food."

The offer is tempting. Way better than three days of solitude and processed food. But still...

"I don't want to impose on your family holiday."

Quinn rolls her eyes. "Please. My mom loves having my friends over. She's been asking when she'll get to meet my roommate anyway." She grabs her phone and starts typing rapidly. "I'm texting her right now."

"Wait—"

"Too late!" She grins triumphantly. "And...sent. 'Mom, my roommate Whitney's plans fell through. Can she join us for Thanksgiving?' She'll say yes. She always does."

Sure enough, Quinn's phone chimes less than a minute later. Her smile widens as she reads the message.

"Mom says, and I quote, 'Of course! I'll make up the guest room. Does she have any food allergies I should know about?'"

The knot in my chest loosens slightly. "That's really sweet of her."

"So it's settled." Quinn bounces slightly on her mattress. "You're spending Thanksgiving with the Hunter family. Fair warning—my brother might be there, and he's kind of annoying, but we can avoid him most of the time."

I haven't met Quinn's brother, but I've heard plenty about him—engineering major, allegedly charming, definitely overprotective. It's still better than the alternative.

"Thank you," I say, genuinely touched by her immediate inclusion. "I really appreciate it."

Quinn waves away my gratitude. "That's what friends are for. Besides, now you can help me run lines for the showcase. Mom and Dad get bored after five minutes."

As Quinn chatters on about her family's Thanksgiving traditions, I let myself relax. Maybe this holiday won't be a total disaster after all. And who knows—maybe a few days away from campus, away from my routine, is exactly what I need to clear my head.

I'm still feeling the emotional whiplash from rehearsal when there's a sharp knock on our door. Quinn springs up from her bed like she's been waiting for this interruption.

"I'll get it!" She bounces over to the door, flicking her messy bun loose so her blonde hair cascades down her shoulders in that effortlessly perfect way I've never been able to achieve.

I stay put on my loft bed, grateful for the elevation and the distance it provides from whatever social situation is about to invade our space. From my perch, I have a perfect view as Quinn swings the door open with a flourish.

"Well, hello there," she purrs, and I immediately know we're in trouble.

Two guys stand in the doorway—Tyler Jenkins and Mike Williams. Great. Just what my emotionally exhausted self needs right now.

"Ladies." Tyler grins, leaning against the doorframe in that practiced casual pose guys think looks cool. His dark hair is artfully tousled, and his varsity jacket announces his status as if anyone on campus could possibly be unaware he's the basketball team captain.

Mike hovers slightly behind him, offering a wave that's surprisingly shy coming from a guy who's built like a linebacker. He was definitely athletic—*and* a good-looking black young man.

"We were just in the neighborhood," Tyler says, which is a ridiculous statement considering we're in an all-girls dorm.

Quinn steps back, gesturing them inside with a dramatic sweep of her arm. "Well, don't just stand there letting all the air conditioning out. Come in!"

They shuffle into our tiny room, which suddenly feels about ten sizes too small. I'm thankful for my loft bed sanctuary as they all cram into the limited floor space below. Quinn perches on the edge of her bed, patting the spot beside her while making eyes at Tyler, who doesn't need to be invited twice.

"So what brings you boys to our neck of the woods?" Quinn asks, twirling a strand of hair around her finger.

Mike glances up at me, offering an awkward smile. "We were heading to the dining hall and thought we'd see if you ladies wanted to join us."

"How thoughtful," I say, not bothering to keep the dryness out of my voice.

Quinn shoots me a look that clearly says *be nice*. "We already ate," she tells them, "but we appreciate the thought."

"Worth a shot." Tyler shrugs, then shifts closer to Quinn. "Actually, there's this party at the Delta house on Friday night. Should be pretty epic. You in?"

Quinn's eyes light up. "A Delta party? Those guys know how to do it right."

"They're flying in a DJ from Atlanta," Tyler continues, clearly pleased with her reaction. "And they've got some seniors with fake IDs making a liquor run tomorrow."

"Sounds amazing," Quinn gushes. She turns toward me. "Whitney, we're going, right?"

Before I can respond, Mike steps closer to my loft bed, looking up at me with those earnest brown eyes. "You should definitely come. It won't be the same without you there."

I resist the urge to roll my eyes—I need to play along if I want to continue the ruse. Anyhow ... Mike has been trying to get my attention since orientation freshman year. He's nice enough—polite, decent grades, friendly smile—but there's just never been any spark. Not like with Jax, where a single text can send electricity buzzing under my skin for hours.

"I don't know," I hedge, picking at a loose thread on my comforter. "I might have plans."

Quinn raises an eyebrow. "What plans? You never mentioned any plans to me."

Thanks for throwing me under the bus, roomie.

Mike's face falls slightly. "Hot date?"

The question catches me off guard. My mind immediately jumps to Jax—his hands, his mouth, the way he looked at me last time, like he was trying to memorize every inch of my skin. We've been texting about meeting up Friday night, but nothing's confirmed yet. Just the usual *"You free?"* followed by my *"Could be"* dance we do.

But then another thought hits me: *what if Jax is seeing other women?* We've never discussed exclusivity. That's not what our arrangement is about. For all I know, he could be texting three other girls the exact same message.

The idea makes my stomach twist uncomfortably. *Why should I sit around waiting for a text when I could be out having fun?*

"Actually," I say, surprising myself, "I don't have anything planned for Friday after all."

Mike's face lights up like I've just handed him the keys to a brand-new car. "For real? So you'll come to the party?"

Quinn gives me a curious look. She knows something's

up—I never change my mind this quickly—but thankfully she doesn't call me out.

"I mean, I've been working hard on this showcase," I reason, more to myself than to anyone else. "I deserve a night off."

"That's the spirit!" Tyler cheers from Quinn's bed. "College is about the experience, not just grades."

"Says the guy on academic probation," Mike teases, and Tyler throws a pillow at him.

"The party starts at ten," Tyler tells Quinn, ignoring his friend. "But a bunch of us are pregaming at my apartment around eight if you want to join."

Quinn practically squeals with delight. "That sounds perfect! We'll be there."

I climb down from my loft, suddenly needing to move, to do something with this restless energy building beneath my skin. "I need to grab some water. Anyone else want some?"

"I'll take one," Mike says quickly, following me to our mini fridge.

As I bend down to grab the water bottles, I feel my

phone vibrate in my back pocket. I ignore it, handing a bottle to Mike instead.

"So," he says, his voice dropping to a more private volume. "I'm really glad you're coming on Friday."

I twist the cap off my water, taking a long drink to delay my response. When I lower the bottle, Mike is still looking at me expectantly, those brown eyes full of hope.

"It should be fun," I say noncommittally.

"Maybe we could hang out, just us, sometime before then?" he ventures. "There's this new coffee place downtown that's supposed to be amazing."

Behind us, Quinn and Tyler are deep in conversation about the party, their heads close together, Quinn's laughter ringing out every few seconds.

My phone vibrates again in my pocket. Twice in two minutes. It's likely Jax, following up on his earlier text. My fingers itch to check it, but I force myself to focus on Mike, who's standing in front of me, real and present, asking me out for coffee.

"Sure," I hear myself say. "Coffee could be nice."

Mike's smile is immediate and genuine. "Dope! How about tomorrow after your last class?"

"I have rehearsal until five," I tell him, already wondering if I'm making a mistake.

"Five-thirty at Roasted Bean?" he suggests. "It's just off campus, near the bookstore."

"I know the place."

My phone vibrates a third time, and this time I can't help but reach for it, pulling it partially out of my pocket just enough to glimpse the screen.

> Jax: Tonight instead of Friday?
>
> Jax: I need to see you
>
> Jax: You up for it? My place at 9?

My heart rate kicks up. Three texts in a row. He never does that.

"Everything okay?" Mike asks, noticing my distraction.

I shove my phone back into my pocket, feeling guilty without knowing exactly why. "Yeah, just my mom," I lie. "Following up about Thanksgiving."

"Cool." Mike takes a swig of his water. "So tomorrow, five-thirty?"

From Quinn's bed, Tyler stands up. "We should head out, bro. We've got that group project meeting at seven."

Mike looks disappointed but nods. "Right, almost forgot." He turns back to me. "Tomorrow, then?"

I nod, pushing thoughts of Jax to the back of my mind. "Tomorrow."

The guys say their goodbyes, Tyler giving Quinn a lingering hug while Mike offers me an awkward wave. As soon as the door closes behind them, Quinn whirls on me.

"Okay, what was that about? You told Mike you're free Friday when I know for a fact you've been hanging on to your phone all week waiting for a text from—*so-called Mike*. What gives?"

I sink onto her bed, suddenly exhausted. "I lied."

"Right, and?"

"I don't know. Maybe I'm tired of waiting around for texts that might never come."

"Right—I knew it! Who is this guy? Are you ever gonna tell me?" Quinn asked, plopping on her bed now.

I quickly think about it. It's probably over by now. "No, he's just a hook-up."

Quinn stares at me for a moment. "So you're going to lead Mike on instead?" Her tone isn't accusatory, just concerned.

"It's just coffee," I say defensively. "And maybe I should be going to parties and having normal college experiences instead of... whatever it is I've been doing."

Quinn sits beside me, bumping my shoulder with hers. "Hey, I'm not judging. If you want to go to the party, great. If you want to grab coffee with Mike, also great. I just don't want to see either of you get hurt."

My phone feels heavy in my pocket, those three unanswered texts burning a hole through the fabric. "I'm not sure what I want anymore."

"Well," Quinn says, standing up and stretching, "You've got about twenty-four hours to figure it out before coffee with Mike. And about five minutes to decide about tonight with the mystery man."

She's right, and that's what scares me. Decisions have consequences. Saying yes to Mike means what? And what about Jax? Do I really want to keep this casual thing going when it's starting to feel less casual by the day?

I pull out my phone again, staring at Jax's texts. Three in a row. *I need to see you.* Not *want* to see you. *Need.*

My thumb hovers over the keyboard as Quinn disappears into our bathroom, giving me privacy for a decision she knows I need to make alone.

SEVEN

Thanksgiving Day

DAVID HUNTER

THE SMELL of turkey and cinnamon fills my mother's kitchen. I'm elbow-deep in bread crumbs and chopped celery, mixing the stuffing the way Mom taught me years ago. It's that one signature recipe she refuses to entrust to anyone else's hands except mine. Something about how I have "the touch." Whatever that means.

"You're going too fast, Davey," Mom scolds, nudging me with her hip as she glides past with a casserole dish. "Folding, not beating. It's not one of your engineering projects."

I slow my pace, watching her flutter around the kitchen like some kind of domestic hummingbird. For a woman who admitted to me just days ago that she's been unhappily married for years, she sure knows how to turn on the holiday charm. But that's my mother—Lara Hunter, master of compartmentalization.

"Where's Dad?" I ask, even though I already know the answer. Same as last year. Same as every holiday.

Mom's shoulders tense for just a fraction of a second before she resumes peeling potatoes. "Conference in Chicago. Very important clients." Her voice takes on that hollow quality it gets whenever she's recycling one of his excuses.

"On Thanksgiving? Again?"

"Well, the world doesn't stop turning just because we're eating turkey, does it?" She shrugs, but I catch the slight tremble in her lower lip before she turns away. "Actually, it's better this way. You know how he gets when there are too many people around."

By "gets," she means miserable, checking his watch every five minutes, and making thinly veiled comments about other people's life choices. Particularly mine.

"Yeah," I say, wiping my hands on a dish towel. "Yeah, I guess so."

I move behind her and place my hands on her shoulders, giving them a gentle squeeze. She leans back against me for just a moment, and I catch a glimpse of the vulnerability she rarely shows.

"Hey, who needs him anyway?" I say. "You've got me—the superior Hunter man."

She laughs, turning to pat my cheek. "That you are, sweetheart. That you are."

I watch Mom bustle around the kitchen, her movements practiced and precise. Every motion has this theatrical quality to it, like she's putting on a show even when no one's watching. Maybe that's what happens when you've spent decades pretending everything's fine.

Damn Dad. He can't even forego business for a family holiday. Not one damn time.

I focus back on the stuffing, crushing a dried bread cube between my fingers until it disintegrates. The crumbs scatter across the mixing bowl like the pieces of our family traditions—fragmented, incomplete, always missing the same vital component.

"Davey, be a dear and check if the wine's chilled enough?" Mom calls from across the kitchen.

"Sure thing."

I open the refrigerator, feeling the cool air against my face. The bottles stand in formation like little soldiers, all lined up for a battle that's been raging longer than I can remember. My mind drifts through the album of family holidays, each one marked by Dad's absence.

My eighth birthday—Dad was in Seattle closing some massive deal.

Christmas when I was twelve—Dad managed to make it home but spent the entire time on conference calls in his study.

My high school graduation—he showed up for the ceremony at least, sat there checking emails on his phone while I walked across the stage.

And the pattern just kept repeating. Year after year. Holiday after holiday. Excuse after excuse.

I grab the wine bottle, testing its temperature against my palm. Cold, just like the hollow feeling that's settled in my chest.

"It's ready," I say, returning to the kitchen island.

Mom nods, wiping her hands on her apron. "Perfect timing. Quinn just texted—she's about twenty minutes out. Says her friend is coming too."

"Friend?"

"Yes, that roommate I told you about. The one who was going to be alone for the holiday. You know your sister—never could stand the thought of someone celebrating alone." Mom smiles. "It'll be nice having a full house for once."

I grunt noncommittally. Great. Another person to witness our dysfunctional family charade.

The thought of Dad snaps back into my mind as I pour myself a glass of wine. *What if there's more to his constant absences than just work? What if all these business trips aren't actually about business at all?*

The idea slides into my brain like a cold snake. *What if Dad has a mistress? Some chick he's been seeing all these years?*

It would explain so much—the missed holidays, the late-night calls he takes in private, the way he barely looks at Mom anymore. The way he's slowly extracted himself from this family piece by piece, year by year.

I take a long sip of wine, letting the acidic tang coat my tongue. It's not like the thought hasn't crossed my mind before, but today it feels more real, more probable. Maybe it's seeing Mom here, putting on the whole

Thanksgiving production single-handedly again, or maybe it's just that I'm old enough now to recognize the patterns.

"Everything okay, sweetie? You look like you're solving calculus in your head." Mom interrupts my thoughts, her hand gentle on my arm.

"Just thinking about Dad." The words slip out before I can filter them.

Her smile falters for just a moment before she recovers. "Well, don't waste your holiday thoughts on him. He made his choice."

There's an edge to her voice I don't often hear—something sharp and knowing. It makes me wonder if she's had the same thoughts I have. If she lies awake at night wondering who else might be sharing her husband's company while she sleeps alone.

"Has he always been like this?" I ask, the wine making me bolder than usual.

Mom pauses, a potato peeler suspended in her hand. "Like what?"

"Absent. Disinterested. Like we're just some obligation he has to check in on occasionally."

She sets the peeler down, and for a moment I think she's going to brush off the question with one of her practiced deflections. Instead, she leans against the counter and meets my eyes.

"Your father wasn't always... like he is now. There was a time when he wanted this life—the house, the kids, the whole picture. But some people aren't built for the long haul, Davey. They want the idea of something more than the reality."

"So why stay?" The question comes out harsher than I intended.

"Twenty-five years is a long time to invest in something just to walk away." She shrugs, but the gesture seems weighted. "Besides, there are different kinds of marriages. Different arrangements."

The implication hangs in the air between us. I feel like I've just been granted access to some adult understanding that was previously off-limits.

"You know, don't you?" I ask quietly. "About... whatever he does when he's away."

Mom picks up her wine glass, takes a sip, and sets it down with deliberate care. "I know enough. And what I don't know, I choose not to investigate."

Jesus. The confirmation settles in my stomach like a stone. All these years, she's known. Or suspected enough that amounts to the same thing.

"How can you just accept that?" My voice cracks a little with the incredulity of it.

"Oh, Davey," she sighs, and suddenly she looks tired—not just holiday-preparation tired but bone-deep exhausted. "Life isn't black and white like you think it is at your age. Sometimes you make compromises to maintain the things that matter."

"What matters about this? He treats you like—"

"Like what? A woman who gets to live in a beautiful home? Who never has to worry about money? Whose children had every advantage?" Her voice is gentle but firm. "Your father may not be the husband I dreamed of, but he gave me the life I wanted in other ways. That's the bargain we struck, even if it wasn't spoken aloud."

I shake my head, disgust and sadness fighting for prominence. "That's not a marriage. That's a business arrangement."

Mom's laugh is soft but without humor. "Maybe all marriages are business arrangements of one kind or another in the end."

I drain my wine glass, needing the burn in my throat to distract from the tightness in my chest. This is exactly why I never want to get into a serious relationship. This slow decay, this mutual disappointment, this silent agreement to pretend things are fine when they're anything but.

Look at them—my parents, the perfect cautionary tale. Dad, who couldn't even be bothered to stick around for Thanksgiving, probably spending it with some other woman while Mom basts the turkey and sets the table with the good china. And Mom, who knows exactly what's happening but has decided the devil she knows is better than the uncertainty of leaving.

Is that what love becomes? A series of betrayals you learn to live with?

No fucking thank you. I'll take my freedom. I'll take no strings attached. I'll take Nikki—no, not even Nikki. Just "Nikki," whoever she really is. A woman I don't fully know, who doesn't fully know me. Safe. Contained. Without the risk of slowly growing to resent each other over turkey dinners and missed holidays.

Mom moves to the oven, checking something inside before closing it again. "Quinn just texted that they're turning onto our street." She glances at me, and her expression softens. "Davey, don't let what your father and I have—or don't have—color your view of relationships. Not everyone makes the choices we did."

"Yeah, because I won't be making those choices at all," I mutter.

She comes over and cups my face in her hands the way she did when I was little. "You say that now. But one day you might meet someone who makes you rethink all those rules you've set for yourself."

I pull away gently. "I doubt it."

The doorbell chimes, announcing Quinn's arrival. Mom's face lights up with genuine joy as she hurries to answer it. I stay in the kitchen, refilling my wine glass and trying to shake off the heaviness of our conversation.

I push away from the kitchen counter, wine glass in hand, and make my way to the living room. The couch calls to me—its soft cushions promising a temporary escape from the weight of my thoughts.

I drop onto the worn leather with a sigh. For a moment, I sit there, swirling the burgundy liquid in my glass, watching it catch the light from Mom's fancy harvest-themed candles. Then I pivot, swinging my legs up and stretching out across the full length of the couch. The leather creaks beneath me.

"That's better," I mumble to myself, taking another sip.

The wine is good—not that I'm any connoisseur, but it slides down smooth and warm. Mom always splurges on the wine for holidays, even when Dad isn't here to appreciate it. Especially when Dad isn't here.

From the front of the house, I hear the door open, followed by my sister's unmistakable squeal. Quinn's voice carries through the house like it always has, high-pitched and excited, still sounding like the twelve-year-old girl who used to follow me around.

"Mom! Oh my god, everything smells amazing!"

I roll my eyes, not bothering to get up. Quinn will make her way through the house like a hurricane, finding everyone in her path. She's always been like that—entering a room and immediately demanding everyone's attention. The golden child. Dad's favorite.

I take another sip, longer this time, letting the alcohol pool in my mouth before swallowing.

The image of Dad seated across from some nameless, faceless woman at a restaurant in Chicago flickers in my mind. *Is he holding her hand across the table? Is he telling her the same jokes he used to tell at our dinner table? Does he look at her the way he never looks at Mom anymore?*

My stomach clenches. I've spent years being angry at my father for his absence, for his disinterest, for his constant criticism of my life choices. But somehow, the idea that he might be straight-up cheating on Mom makes everything worse. It transforms him from merely a shitty dad to something more insidious.

"Is it possible to respect someone less than zero?" I mutter to my wine glass.

I hear more voices from the entryway—Quinn introducing someone, Mom's warm welcome. *Right, the roommate.* I'd almost forgotten about our holiday guest. Another person to witness our family's particular brand of dysfunction. Lucky her.

My phone buzzes in my pocket. I fish it out, expecting a text from one of my engineering buddies, probably something about their own holiday disasters. Instead, I see a name that makes my pulse quicken slightly.

Nikki.

I open the message.

Thanksgiving Day

> Nikki: Happy Thanksgiving. Hope it doesn't suck too much. I'm thinking about that thing you did last time...

Heat floods my face as I remember exactly which "thing" she's referring to. For a brief moment, the memory drowns out my cynical thoughts about my parents' marriage. Nikki—or whatever her real name is—represents everything good about my approach to relationships. No complications. No disappointments. No slow, painful descent into mutual resentment. Just two people enjoying each other's bodies without the messy emotional baggage.

I type back:

> Jax: It definitely sucks. Wish I was doing that thing to you right now instead.

Send.

I lock the phone and set it on my chest, staring up at the ceiling. Mom's antique chandelier needs dusting. I wonder if Dad even knows things like that anymore—the small domestic details of the home he supposedly lives in. *Does he notice the water stain in the corner of the dining room ceiling? Does he know Mom replaced the microwave three months ago?*

Does he care?

The sound of heels clicking against hardwood grows closer. Quinn, no doubt, coming to find her big brother. I don't move, don't sit up, don't make any effort to appear welcoming. Let her see me as I am—horizontally drinking wine at one in the afternoon, contemplating the wreckage of our parents' marriage.

"There you are." Quinn's voice comes from the doorway. "Typical Davey, lounging around while everyone else does the work."

I lift my wineglass in a mock toast without looking at her. "Someone's got to test the wine. Making sure it's not poisoned. You're welcome."

"Get up, you lazy ass. Come say hello properly."

"I'm comfortable."

"David." There's that tone she uses when she's trying to sound authoritative. It never works on me, but she keeps trying. "I brought my roommate. The one I told you about?"

She's never told me about her...

"You could at least pretend to be socialized."

I take another sip, still not looking her way. "Did I miss the part where I asked you to bring a stranger to our family dysfunction display?"

"Stop being a jerk. Whitney's cool, and she was going to be alone for Thanksgiving."

Whitney. The name registers somewhere in the back of my mind. Quinn mentions her roommate occasionally in our sporadic texts and calls—something about them both being in drama together. An actress, then. Great. Another performer to add to our family's holiday theater production.

"I'm sure Whitney will be just fine without meeting me," I say, still fixated on the chandelier. "I'm not exactly bringing my A-game today."

Quinn sighs dramatically. I can practically hear her eyes rolling. "Fine. Wallow in whatever mood this is. But dinner's in an hour, and Mom expects you at the table, so..." She trails off, her heels clicking back down the hallway.

That's another reason I keep things casual with Nikki. We can't disappoint each other if we never expect anything in the first place. We can't grow to resent what we never had. It's perfect in its simplicity. Clean. Uncomplicated.

So why does it sometimes feel so empty?

I open my eyes and stare at the ceiling again. I should get up. I should go help Mom. I should greet Quinn properly and meet her roommate and be the good son, the good brother. But I can't seem to make myself move. The weight of what I've learned today—the confirmation of Dad's betrayal, the knowledge that Mom has been silently enduring it for who knows how long—it pins me to the couch like a physical force.

How do you go through the motions of a family holiday when you've just been shown that the foundation of that family is built on lies?

I lift my empty wine glass, studying it as if it might contain answers. But there's nothing there—just the faint residue of red along the bottom, slowly drying into a stain.

Like my father's absence. Like my mother's quiet resignation. Like all the small betrayals that accumulate over time until you wake up one day and realize your family isn't what you thought it was at all.

I set the glass down on the coffee table and close my eyes again, determined to stay right where I am until absolutely necessary. Quinn will find me eventually. Dinner will be served. The holiday will proceed.

And I'll get through it the same way I get through everything else these days—one moment at a time, expecting nothing, protecting myself from the inevitable disappointment that comes with caring too much.

EIGHT

What the Fuck?

WHITNEY BARNES

I STAND in the driveway of the Hunter residence, clutching the small gift bag containing a bottle of wine I splurged on for Mrs. Hunter. The house is nothing short of magnificent—a sprawling two-story colonial with perfect symmetry, bay windows, and white columns framing the deep burgundy front door. Nothing like my mom's cluttered apartment back in Chicago.

"Come on," Quinn tugs at my arm, breaking my trance. "Mom's gone all out this year. Wait till you see inside."

My heels click against the cobblestone walkway as we approach. Quinn doesn't bother knocking, just throws the door open like she owns the place—which, technically, she does.

"Holy shit," I whisper under my breath as we step inside.

The foyer opens to a vaulted ceiling with a crystal chandelier that catches the afternoon sunlight, scattering tiny rainbows across cream-colored walls. To the right, a formal living room with furniture that looks like it's never been sat on. To the left, a dining room with a mahogany table already set with china that probably costs more than my entire wardrobe. The smell of roasting turkey, sweet potatoes, and something buttery and divine permeates the air.

"Your house is..." I struggle to find the right words.

"Pretentious? Over the top?" Quinn laughs.

"Beautiful," I finish. "It's beautiful."

A wall of family photos catches my attention—Quinn through various ages, school portraits, vacation snapshots. And there's another face that appears frequently: a boy, then a teenager, Quinn's brother, I assume. I've heard stories, but never seen pictures.

"Girls? Is that you?" A warm voice calls from somewhere deeper in the house.

"In the flesh!" Quinn yells back. "Whitney's with me!"

What the Fuck?

I follow Quinn through the house, taking in the plush carpet beneath my feet, the tasteful artwork on the walls, the spotless surfaces. My apartment growing up had water stains on the ceiling and secondhand furniture. Mom did her best, but this... this is another world.

We enter the kitchen, a chef's dream with marble countertops, stainless steel appliances, and an island large enough to seat six. Dishes in various stages of preparation cover every surface, and standing in the middle of it all is Lara Hunter, looking like she stepped out of a Williams-Sonoma catalog in her apron and perfectly styled blonde hair.

"Whitney!" she exclaims, wiping her hands on a dish towel before enveloping me in a hug that smells like vanilla and expensive perfume. "I'm so glad Quinn convinced you to join us. No one should be alone on Thanksgiving."

"Thank you for having me, Mrs. Hunter," I say, offering the wine. "It's not much, but—"

"It's perfect, and please call me Lara." She takes the bag. "Quinn, show Whitney where she can put her things. Dinner's at four, but appetizers are in the family room if you're hungry."

As Quinn leads me back through the house, I notice more details—crown molding, recessed lighting, hardwood floors that gleam. The family room has a stone fireplace with actual flames crackling, oversized leather couches, and a TV that covers nearly an entire wall.

Quinn leaves for a moment, while I'm still in awe. When she reappears, she grabs my arm.

"You can put your coat in my room," Quinn says, leading me up a curved staircase.

I follow her down a hallway lined with more family photos. Quinn's childhood bedroom is exactly as I'd imagined—pink walls, dance trophies, posters of boy bands. A far cry from my teenage room with its hand-me-down furniture and walls I wasn't allowed to paint.

"Your house is incredible," I say, setting my overnight bag on the window seat.

Quinn flops onto her bed. "It's just a house. You should see my dad's place in Aspen."

The doorbell rings before I can respond.

"That's Aunt Lisa and the brats," Quinn jumps up. "Come on, they're actually cool."

What the Fuck?

Back downstairs, the front door opens to more Hunters—a woman who looks like Lara but with darker hair, and two teenagers who immediately high-five Quinn.

"Lisa!" Lara embraces her sister. "So glad you made it. Traffic wasn't too bad?"

"Not terrible," Lisa says, unwinding a scarf from her neck. "Oh, is this Quinn's roommate? Hello, dear!"

Before I know it, I'm being hugged by Quinn's aunt and introduced to her cousins, Emma and Tyler. The foyer fills with animated conversation, laughter, and the rustle of coats being removed.

"David!" Lara calls out. "Your aunt and cousins are here!"

There's movement from the family room, and I hear a familiar voice respond, "Coming."

My stomach does a little flip at the deep timbre. Something about it triggers a memory, but I can't place it. From the corner of my eye, I see someone rise from the couch and head toward us.

Quinn grabs my hand suddenly. "Come meet your favorite aunt and your favorite cousins!"

"Our *only* aunt and *only* cousins..." I hear him say.

She pulls me toward the growing cluster of people in the foyer, and I'm smiling, ready to make a good impression, when a tall figure enters from the other direction.

My heart stops.

Blonde hair. Hazel eyes. The jawline I've traced with my fingers countless times in the dark.

Jax.

No, not Jax. David. Quinn's brother David.

My *Jax* is David Hunter.

The room seems to tilt on its axis as our eyes lock. His face drains of color, pupils dilating in shock.

"What the fuck?" he mouths silently.

My knees nearly buckle. I'm Nikki to him. The fake name I use for hook-ups. For men I never intend to see in the light of day. For casual sex with no strings, no real names, no complications.

Except now there are complications. A fucking avalanche of them.

I'm standing in his family home. I've been sleeping with my best friend's brother for months.

David's eyes are wide, his body frozen in place even as his aunt Lisa throws her arms around him. He hugs her mechanically, his gaze never leaving mine.

Quinn is chattering away, oblivious to the nuclear bomb that's just detonated in her foyer. "Whitney, these are my cousins Emma and Tyler, and my aunt Lisa—and that's my brother David, the engineering genius."

Engineering?

David finally manages to break eye contact, turning to hug his cousins. I can see the tension in his shoulders, the stiffness in his movements. He's as shocked as I am.

"Nice to meet you all," I say, my voice sounding distant and hollow to my own ears. I force a smile, hoping no one notices how badly my hands are shaking.

Quinn pulls me closer to David. "David, this is my roommate Whitney I've been telling you about. The one who's going to be famous one day."

David's eyes flash back to mine, and I see the pieces clicking together in his mind. Whitney. Nikki. Quinn's roommate. The girl he's been fucking.

"Whitney," he says, the name strange on his tongue as he extends his hand to me. It's the hand that's explored every inch of my body. But here we are, pretending to be strangers. "Nice to finally meet you."

His palm is warm against mine, the contact sending electricity up my arm. We hold the handshake a beat too long, both of us unable to process what's happening.

"You too," I manage. "I've heard a lot about you."

His mouth twitches. "Likewise."

The tension between us is so thick I'm certain everyone can feel it. But they don't. The family continues talking, laughing, moving toward the kitchen as David and I remain locked in our private nightmare.

Quinn glances between us, her brow furrowing. "What the fuck is going on?"

"What?" David asks, too quickly.

"Nothing," I say at the same time.

Quinn's eyes narrow. "You two … do you know each other or something?"

David clears his throat. "No, just… thought she looked familiar for a second."

Quinn crosses her arms. "And Whitney, your face is doing that thing it does when you're hiding something.

The same face you make when I ask where you disappear to some nights."

My cheeks burn. David shifts his weight uncomfortably.

Quinn's eyes suddenly widen. Her mouth forms a perfect O of realization. "No fucking way," she whispers. "No. Fucking. Way." She points at David, then me, then back at David. "What the fuck is going on?"

The three of us stand frozen in the foyer as the rest of the family continues their Thanksgiving celebrations, blissfully unaware of the bomb that's just exploded.

"No fucking way," Quinn repeats, her voice rising. "You two—oh shit!"

I open my mouth, but no words come out. My brain is short-circuiting. Every neural pathway is scrambling to process this impossible situation. Jax is David. David is Jax. The guy I've been sleeping with for months is my best friend's brother.

The dining room chatter feels distant, like it's happening in another dimension. In this one, there's just the three of us, locked in this excruciating triangle of revelation.

Quinn's eyes dart between us, piecing things together with frightening speed. "Is my brother your mystery hookup?"

David finally moves, reaching out to grab my arm. His fingers press into my skin—the same grip that's guided me in his bedroom countless times.

"We have to talk," he says, his voice low and urgent. Those hazel eyes I've gazed into in the dark now look at me with panic.

Quinn steps closer, jaw set in determination. "Oh hell no. Whatever's happening, I want to know right now."

"Quinn," David says sharply, turning to his sister. "Please. Just give me and Whitney a moment to process this."

"Process what exactly?" Quinn demands, crossing her arms.

David rubs his forehead, the gesture so familiar it makes my stomach clench. "This is... complicated. And not something we should hash out in the foyer while the whole family is here."

Quinn stares at him hard, then at me. I see hurt flashing across her face, but also confusion. After what feels like an eternity, her shoulders drop slightly.

"Fine," she says, taking a step back. "But when you're done with whatever this is, I expect a full explanation. Both of you."

David nods, his grip on my arm loosening but not letting go. He guides me away from the foyer, past the kitchen where Lara is laughing with Lisa, past the living room where the cousins have settled in front of the TV.

My legs move automatically, following him through a hallway I haven't seen yet. I feel like I'm floating outside my body, watching this disaster unfold from somewhere near the ceiling.

This can't be happening. Not today. Not here.

We reach a door at the end of the hall. David opens it, ushers me inside, and closes it behind us. It's an office—dark wood furniture, bookshelves lining the walls, a leather chair behind an imposing desk.

The click of the door closing sounds final, like a judge's gavel. Silence falls between us, thick and suffocating.

I look at him—really look at him—in proper lighting for the first time. Our encounters have always been in the dim glow of his apartment, shadows concealing details. But here, I see everything. The tiny scar above his right eyebrow. The way his blonde hair has subtle darker strands near the roots. The exact shade of his hazel eyes—green with flecks of gold and brown.

"Nikki—" he starts, then stops himself. "Whitney."

My name on his lips sounds wrong. I've been Nikki to him for months. Just as he's been Jax to me.

"Don't call me that," I say, my voice barely audible.

"What—Nikki or Whitney?" His brow furrows.

"Either." I wrap my arms around myself. "I don't know. This is insane."

He runs his hands through his hair, a gesture I've seen countless times post-sex when he's thinking or stressed. "You're Quinn's roommate. How did I not see this coming? She talks about you all the time."

"She talks about her brother David," I say. "Not Jax. I never made the connection."

He paces in front of the desk, his movements agitated. "Shit. Shit, shit, shit."

"My thoughts exactly," I mutter.

David stops pacing and faces me. "We need to figure out what to tell Quinn."

"The truth?" I suggest weakly.

"That I've been fucking her roommate for three months? That'll go over great at Thanksgiving dinner." He pinches the bridge of his nose.

What the Fuck?

The crude way he phrases it stings, even though it's accurate. That's all we've been to each other—a physical release with no strings attached. At least, that's what we told ourselves.

"This is exactly why I use a different name," I say. "To avoid messy situations."

"Well, here we are anyway," he replies, gesturing between us. "In the messiest situation possible."

I sink into one of the leather chairs facing the desk, my legs unable to support me anymore. "What are we going to do?"

David leans against the desk, facing me. For a moment, he looks just like he does in his apartment—casual, intense, focused entirely on me. It sends an inappropriate flutter through my body that I immediately try to squash.

"We tell her we met online, used fake names, and had no idea about the connection until today," he says. "It's the truth."

"And then what?" I ask. "We just... stop seeing each other?"

The question hangs in the air between us. I didn't mean to phrase it that way—like there was a decision to be made, like continuing was even an option. But now that it's out there, I find myself holding my breath for his answer.

David's eyes meet mine, and something passes between us—something deeper than the physical connection we've shared. For the first time, I wonder if he's felt it too—that nagging sense that what we've been doing was evolving into something more than just hookups.

"I guess that would be the sensible thing," he says slowly.

I nod, ignoring the sinking feeling in my chest. "Right." I stare at him. "Of course it does. You're Quinn's brother. My best friend's brother. We can't just keep—"

"I know, I know," he interrupts, pushing off the desk to pace. "I'm not thinking clearly. Finding out that Nikki is actually my sister's roommate Whitney has kind of scrambled my brain."

"Mine too," I admit.

He stops pacing and faces me again. "Can I just say... this is not how I pictured meeting the *real* you."

A bubble of hysterical laughter escapes me. "You pictured meeting the real me?"

He has the grace to look embarrassed. "Maybe. Sometimes. After you'd leave, I'd wonder who you really were."

This confession lands like a thunderbolt. All those nights I'd sneak out of his apartment, assuming he rolled over and fell asleep without a second thought about the woman who'd just left his bed. All those times I'd wondered if I was just a body to him, a convenient arrangement.

"I wondered about you too," I admit quietly.

We stand in silence for a moment, the revelation settling between us. For months, we'd maintained the charade of casual sex with fake names and no strings, while secretly wondering about each other's real lives.

"Quinn's going to hate us," I say eventually.

"Quinn's going to be shocked," he corrects. "Then upset. Then she'll process. Then she'll be fine."

"You sound awfully confident about that."

He smiles slightly. "I've been dealing with my sister's dramatics for twenty-two years. Trust me on this one."

Trust. There's that word. Have I been trusting him all along without realizing it? Trusting him with my body, with my safety, with the parts of myself I could share even while hiding behind a fake name?

"We should go back out there," I say, glancing at the door. "Before they send a search party."

David nods, but neither of us moves. We're suspended in this moment, on the precipice of something new and terrifying. Once we walk out that door, everything changes. Our carefully constructed fantasy world crumbles, replaced by the messy reality of real names, real connections, real consequences.

"Whitney," he says my name deliberately, testing it out.

"David," I respond, doing the same.

We stare at each other, relearning faces we already know by heart.

"Ready?" he asks finally, reaching for the doorknob.

I take a deep breath and nod, even though I'm anything but ready.

NINE

#HookupNow

DAVID HUNTER

MY HEART HAMMERS in my chest as I follow Whitney—not Nikki, Whitney—down the hallway to Quinn's room. Every part of me wants to reach out and touch her, to confirm she's real. The same woman who's been setting my sheets on fire for months is my little sister's roommate? The universe has a sick sense of humor.

I watch her walk ahead of me, those familiar curves now seeming like a forbidden landscape. Her short black curls bounce with each step, and I fight the memory of how they felt brushing against my chest just three nights ago.

"This is fucked up," I mutter under my breath.

Whitney glances over her shoulder, those deep brown

eyes flashing with the same confusion I feel. "You're telling me," she murmurs. "Jax."

The name lands like a slap. "It's David." The words taste strange. All those nights, all those text messages signed with a name that isn't even mine.

She stops walking suddenly, and I nearly collide with her. For a split second, we're too close. Her scent hits me —coconut and something spicy—and my body responds on instinct. I take a deliberate step back, putting distance between us.

"I can't believe this is happening," she says. "Of all the guys in all the world..."

"You had to be roommates with my sister." The absurdity of it makes me want to laugh, but nothing about this feels funny.

We reach Quinn's door, and I hesitate before turning the knob. Our fingers brush accidentally as we both reach for it, and the electricity is still there, damn it. Whitney jerks her hand back like she's been shocked.

I push open the door to find Quinn pacing her childhood bedroom, her blonde hair whipping around as she turns to face us.

"What the actual hell?" Quinn's voice cuts through the tension. Her green eyes narrow as she looks between us. "How long has this been going on?"

I close the door behind us, leaning against it. Being in this small space with Whitney is torture. I can't look at her without remembering how she tastes.

"Three months," I answer, keeping my voice even.

"Four," Whitney corrects, and our eyes meet briefly.

Quinn throws her hands up. "Fantastic. My brother and my best friend have been fucking for four months, and neither of you thought to mention it?"

"We didn't know," Whitney says, sinking onto the edge of Quinn's bed. "I knew him as Jax. He knew me as Nikki."

"Fake names? Seriously?" Quinn looks at me like I'm fifteen again, caught sneaking out of the house. "That's so sleazy, David."

I cross my arms over my chest. "It was mutual. We both wanted anonymity."

"Because you're both so famous?" Quinn sneers.

"Because we both wanted something uncomplicated," I

snap back. The frustration builds in my chest. I don't need my little sister's judgment right now.

"Well, congratulations. You've created the most complicated situation possible." Quinn flops down into her desk chair.

Whitney sits with her hands clasped between her knees, looking smaller than I've ever seen her. It's strange—I've seen her naked, watched her come apart underneath me, but I've never seen her vulnerable like this.

"How did you even meet?" Quinn demands.

I run a hand through my hair, tugging slightly. "HookupNow app."

Quinn's eyes widen. "That trash app? The one that's basically for anonymous sex?"

"It's not trash," Whitney defends weakly. "It's just... straightforward."

"Jesus Christ." Quinn shakes her head. "And neither of you ever thought to share real details about yourselves? Like, I don't know, where you go to school? Your real names?"

"That was the point," I say. "No attachments, no details."

Quinn looks at Whitney with something like betrayal in her eyes. "You've been telling me for months how you don't have time for dating, how you're focused on your career. Meanwhile, you're hooking up with my brother?"

"I didn't know he was your brother!" Whitney's voice rises. "And I haven't been dating. We weren't dating. It was just…"

"Sex," I finish for her, and something twists in my gut when I say it out loud.

Quinn studies me for a long moment, her expression shifting to something more calculating. "Wait. Are you catching feelings, Davey?"

The childhood nickname makes me bristle. "No."

"Then why do you look like someone just canceled Christmas?" She turns to Whitney. "And you. I know that look. You're not as unaffected as you want us to believe."

"Can we not do this right now?" Whitney pleads. "Your mom is downstairs expecting us for Thanksgiving dinner, and we're up here having the most awkward conversation of my life."

Quinn ignores her. "Listen, David. Whitney doesn't *do*

relationships. She's made that very clear to every guy who's ever tried."

I feel my jaw tighten. "I'm not trying anything. We had an arrangement. That's all."

"Good. Because you'd be wasting your time." Quinn stands up and paces again. "In fact, didn't you just have a date with Mike Williams last weekend?" she asks Whitney.

The question hits me like a sucker punch. Mike Williams? The football star whose face is plastered all over campus? Something hot and ugly unfurls in my chest.

Whitney's eyes widen. "Quinn, that wasn't—"

"The wide receiver?" I interrupt, my voice coming out harder than I intended. "Seriously?"

Whitney shoots Quinn a look I can't interpret. "It wasn't a date. We were at the same party."

"He drove you home," Quinn says pointedly. "And he asked for your number."

"And I gave it to him," Whitney admits, not meeting my eyes.

The knowledge shouldn't bother me. It's not like we're exclusive. Hell, we don't even know each other's real names until today. But it does bother me. It bothers me a lot.

"Good for you," I say, forcing a casual tone. "Football players are definitely more your type than engineers."

Whitney's head snaps up. "You don't know my type."

"Clearly not." The bitterness in my voice surprises even me.

Quinn looks between us, realization dawning on her face. "Oh my God. You are catching feelings. Both of you."

"I'm not catching anything," I insist.

"Me neither," Whitney says too quickly.

Quinn laughs, but it's not a happy sound. "This is amazing. My brother and my best friend, both allergic to relationships, somehow managed to develop feelings while pretending not to know each other."

"There are no feelings," I say firmly, even as I feel something dangerous stirring inside me. "We had fun. Now it's over."

Whitney flinches slightly at my words.

"It has to be over," I continue, looking directly at her now. "This is too weird."

Quinn snorts. "Yeah, move on, David. Whitney certainly is. Mike's been texting her non-stop."

"Quinn, stop it," Whitney pleads.

But I'm already backing toward the door. "Message received. You should definitely go for Mike. He's got a bright future ahead of him." I can hear the jealousy in my voice and hate myself for it.

"I don't need your permission," Whitney says, her voice gaining strength. "And I don't owe you explanations. Like you said, it was just sex."

Her words sting more than they should. I open my mouth to reply, but Quinn cuts me off.

"You two need to figure this out before dinner, because Mom will absolutely notice if you're both acting weird." She points at me. "And you, dear brother, have the worst poker face on the planet when you're upset."

"I'm not upset," I lie. "Why would I be upset that the woman I've been sleeping with for four months is already moving on to someone else? That's the whole point of what we were doing."

Whitney stands up suddenly. "You don't get to do that. You don't get to act jealous when you're the one who insisted on all the rules."

"I'm not jealous," I say, even as the thought of her with Mike makes me want to put my fist through a wall.

"Good," Quinn interjects. "Because Whitney deserves someone who wants more than just hookups. And clearly, that's not you."

I stare at my sister, feeling betrayed. "You know nothing about what I want."

"I know you told Mom just this morning that you never want to get married," Quinn counters. "That relationships aren't your thing."

Whitney's expression shifts slightly at this information, something like resignation settling in her features.

"See? You guys are perfect for each other," Quinn continues sarcastically. "Both allergic to commitment, both lying to yourselves. It's a match made in heaven."

"Are we done here?" I ask, my hand on the doorknob. "Because I'd rather eat dinner with our boring Dad than continue this conversation."

Quinn waves her hand dismissively. "Yeah, go. Just act normal downstairs."

I turn to leave but pause when Whitney speaks.

"David." My real name in her voice does something to me. "What happens now?"

I look at her—really look at her—for the first time since we discovered each other's identities. Those lips I've kissed a hundred times. Those eyes that have looked down at me in the dark. This woman who has somehow crawled under my skin without me noticing.

"I think Quinn's right," I answer honestly. "We should both move on."

I SLAM my door so hard the wood frame shudders. My childhood bedroom—untouched since high school—closes around me like a time capsule. Trophies from swim meets line the shelves, engineering competition medals hang from the corkboard, and that stupid "Hunter Boys" pennant Dad got made when Quinn and I were kids dangles from a push pin.

Lock engaged. Barricade in place.

I pace the cramped space between my twin bed and the desk, blood rushing in my ears. My heartbeat hammers against my ribcage like it's trying to escape. Four months. Four fucking months I've been sleeping with my sister's roommate without knowing it.

"Goddammit!"

I grab the nearest thing—my second-place robotics trophy from junior year—and hurl it against the far wall. It connects with a satisfying crack, the little gold-plated robot arm snapping off and skittering across the hardwood floor.

"Mike Williams," I growl, reaching for another trophy. "Football star. Campus hero."

The swim team MVP award flies next, smashing against my old desk lamp.

What was I expecting? That Whitney would be sitting around pining for our next hookup while I was doing the same? That's not how this works. That was never the deal. We agreed: no attachments, no expectations, no explanations.

So why does my chest feel like someone's taken a sledgehammer to it?

"Fucking HookupNow," I mutter, kicking at my backpack sprawled on the floor. The stupid app that promised uncomplicated encounters. Swipe right, meet up, get off, go home. Simple.

Except nothing about this feels simple anymore.

I drop heavily onto my bed, head in my hands. The memory of Whitney—no, Nikki—from three nights ago floods my mind without permission. Her body moving over mine in the darkness of my apartment, those soft curls tickling my face as she leaned down to kiss me. The way she laughed when I pulled her against me afterward, both of us sweaty and spent.

"It was *just* sex," I tell the empty room, but the words sound hollow even to my own ears.

Just sex doesn't make you text each other stupid memes during the day. Just sex doesn't have you saving the last slice of pizza because you know she'll be hungry after. Just sex doesn't have you lying awake wondering what she's doing when she's not with you.

I stand suddenly, snatch my third-place state championship medal from the wall and send it sailing across the room. It hits my old chemistry textbook with an unsatisfying thud before dropping to the floor.

"What the hell is wrong with me?" I ask no one in particular.

This isn't supposed to be happening. I don't do relationships. I don't do feelings. I don't do jealousy.

Yet here I am, destroying my childhood bedroom because Whitney might be seeing Mike Williams. Mike with his perfect spiral throws and NFL prospects. Mike who probably doesn't need fake names and hookup apps to get women into bed.

The thought of his hands on her makes something primal and ugly rear up inside me.

I grab another trophy—regional science fair, honorable mention—and drive it into the trash can with enough force to dent the metal side.

For the first time since high school, I wish this room still had the punching bag Dad installed after I got into that fight sophomore year. I need somewhere to channel this energy, this rage that doesn't make any sense. I'm not supposed to care who Whitney sleeps with. **That was the whole point.**

A soft knock at the door interrupts my destruction tour.

"David?" My mom's voice, muffled through the wood. "Dinner's almost ready, sweetheart."

I freeze mid-reach for another trophy. "I'll be down in a minute, Mom."

"Is everything okay in there? I heard some banging."

I survey the wreckage of my accomplishments scattered across the floor. "Yeah, just... looking for something."

I listen to her footsteps retreat down the hallway before collapsing back onto the bed.

And now I have to sit across the dinner table from Whitney—the woman I've been fantasizing about for months—and pretend I don't know what she sounds like when she comes. Pretend I haven't memorized every curve of her body. Pretend I don't care that some football jock is texting her "non-stop."

I snatch my phone from my pocket, open the HookupNow app, and delete it with a vicious swipe. The action brings me no relief.

This isn't happening because of some stupid app. This is happening because I broke my own rules. Somewhere between the first night and the last, I started caring. Started looking forward to our conversations as much as the sex. Started wondering what it might be like to wake up next to her without one of us having to sneak away.

"Pathetic," I mutter, pressing the heels of my hands against my eyes until I see stars.

Dad's voice echoes in my head: "Relationships are a trap, son. They start with passion and end with paperwork."

I thought I was being smart, following his example in reverse—all passion, no paperwork. No names, no histories, no future plans. Just two bodies finding pleasure in the darkness.

But bodies aren't machines. They come with hearts attached.

I grab a pillow and press it against my face, letting out the most muffled scream I can manage. The childishness of the action isn't lost on me, but it helps—marginally.

My phone buzzes with a text. For a wild second, I think it might be Whitney, but it's just Quinn.

> Quinn: Mom says come down now.
> Stop being a drama queen.

Typical Quinn, direct and unsympathetic. But she's right. This isn't the time or place for whatever emotional breakdown I'm having. I need to get it together, put on my game face, and get through this dinner.

I stand up, straightening my shirt and running a hand through my disheveled hair. The floor is littered with the physical evidence of my accomplishments, now broken and scattered—a fitting metaphor for how I feel inside.

As I bend to pick up the robotics trophy arm, another text comes through.

> Quinn: And just so you know, Whitney is freaking out too. But she's handling it like an adult.

The message stings exactly as Quinn intended it to. Whitney is freaking out too. The image of her sitting downstairs, composed and polite while I'm up here throwing a tantrum, makes shame crawl up my spine.

I set the broken trophy piece on my desk and take a steadying breath. One dinner. I can handle one dinner across the table from her. I've negotiated group projects with people I can't stand. I've given presentations to rooms full of skeptical professors. I can sit at a table with the woman who's turned my world upside down and pretend everything's normal.

As I unlock my door and step into the hallway, I catch a glimpse of my reflection in the bathroom mirror across the way. I look exactly like what I am—a man who just realized he's been lying to himself for months.

I've been so focused on not becoming my father that I've built my life around avoiding his mistakes. Don't get attached. Don't make promises. Don't let anyone close enough to hurt you when they leave.

But as I move toward the stairs, toward Whitney and whatever complicated mess awaits us at the dinner table, I wonder if I've been making my own mistakes all along.

TEN

Out For A Drink

WHITNEY BARNES

I STARE out the dorm window, watching raindrops race down the glass. It's been two weeks since Thanksgiving dinner from hell, and I still can't shake the hollow feeling in my chest. Two weeks since I discovered "Jax" was actually David—Quinn's brother. Two weeks of silence from both sides.

"Whitney? Earth to Whitney?" Quinn waves her hand in front of my face.

I blink, returning to our room. "Sorry, what?"

Quinn rolls her eyes, tossing her blonde hair over her shoulder. "I asked if you wanted coffee before rehearsal."

"Yeah. Sure." My responses have been automatic lately.

I'm going through the motions like someone programmed me to function without feeling.

Quinn studies me, her green eyes narrowing. "You're still weird."

"I'm fine."

"You haven't been fine since Thanksgiving." She crosses her arms. "Look, I get it was awkward finding out you've been hooking up with my brother, but it's been two weeks. Move on already."

Easy for her to say. She doesn't know what it felt like to lock eyes with David across her mother's living room and have my entire world flip upside down. To realize the guy I'd been naked with countless times was my best friend's brother. The shame, the shock, the bizarre betrayal even though neither of us had actually betrayed the other.

"I *am* moving on," I lie, grabbing my script from the desk. "I'm focused on the play. Professor Michaels said the scouts from Regional Theatre Company might attend opening night."

Quinn brightens instantly. "God, could you imagine? Getting scouted while still in college? That would be everything."

I nod mechanically. Before Thanksgiving, that possibility would have set my heart racing. Now, even my dreams feel distant, like they belong to someone else.

"Let's grab that coffee," I say, forcing a smile. "I need the caffeine if I'm going to nail this rehearsal."

THE STAGE LIGHTS beat down on me as I recite my lines in the empty theater. Professor Winters and the crew are on a fifteen-minute break, but I've stayed behind, determined to get this monologue right. My character is supposed to be heartbroken, furious at her lover's betrayal.

At least that feels authentic.

"He loved me once," I say to the empty seats. "Or did I imagine that too? Another fantasy I constructed to make myself believe someone could actually want me—all of me, not just pieces."

I pace across the stage, letting my voice rise with emotion. "And now I'm supposed to, what? Forgive you? Forget how your lies tore through me like—"

Movement in the back of the theater catches my eye. I freeze mid-sentence, squinting past the blinding stage lights. Three silhouettes have entered, hovering near the back row. My heart rate spikes.

Is that...David?

My mouth goes dry. I've imagined seeing him again a thousand times. *What would I say? Would he speak first? Would we pretend not to know each other?* I've rehearsed every scenario except the one where I'm literally in the middle of rehearsal when he shows up.

The figures move closer, emerging from the shadows.

Not David.

Mike Williams strides down the aisle, his linebacker shoulders taking up space even in the cavernous theater. Tyler Jenkins follows behind him, both men dressed in university athletic gear.

"Don't stop on our account," Mike calls out, flashing that smile that melts half the female population on campus.

I exhale slowly, surprised by the disappointment washing through me. "We're on break."

"That didn't sound like a break to me," Mike says, reaching the edge of the stage. "Sounded like you were tearing somebody a new one up there."

Tyler laughs. "Yeah, remind me never to piss you off, Barnes."

I force a smile, tucking my script under my arm. "What brings you guys here? Quinn's not around—she went to grab coffee."

"Actually," Mike says, leaning against the stage, "I came to see you."

My eyebrows lift. Mike Williams is gorgeous—six-foot-four, with warm brown skin, a dazzling smile, and NFL prospects. Under normal circumstances, I'd be thrilled by his attention. Now I just feel...nothing.

"Oh?" I manage.

"Been trying to get you to agree to a date all semester," he says with an easy confidence. "Figured I'd try my luck in person since you keep dodging my texts."

Have I been dodging his texts? I vaguely remember Quinn mentioning something about Mike asking about me, but I've been so caught up in my own head lately.

The stage door bangs open and Quinn appears, balancing two coffee cups. "Mike! Tyler! What are you guys doing here?" Her voice carries that excited lilt she gets around attractive men.

"Watching your roommate kill it," Tyler says with a grin.

Quinn hands me my coffee and gives me a meaningful look I can't quite interpret. "She is amazing, isn't she? Leading lady material for sure."

Mike keeps his eyes on me. "No doubt."

The air feels charged, and I realize I should respond, should say something flirty or clever. That's what the old Whitney would do—the Whitney who hooked up with a stranger from a dating app and kept going back for more because it was fun and uncomplicated.

"Thanks for stopping by," I say instead, taking a sip of coffee to avoid further conversation.

Quinn jumps in, saving me from my awkward silence. "We should all hang out after rehearsal. Get drinks at McCaffrey's?"

"Perfect," Mike agrees instantly. "We'll catch up with you ladies around eight?"

I nod, not trusting myself to speak. Quinn chatters excitedly as the guys leave, making plans and promising to bring friends.

When they're gone, she whirls on me. "What is wrong with you? Mike Williams is practically drooling over you and you're acting like he asked for directions to the library."

I shrug, setting down my coffee cup. "I'm just focused on the play right now."

"Bullshit." Quinn's voice drops to a whisper as other cast members begin returning. "Is this about David? Because I told you—he doesn't *do* relationships. Whatever was happening between you two was never going to be anything serious."

Her words sting more than they should. "I know that."

"Then stop moping and get back out there! Mike is hot, single, and interested. What more could you want?"

What more could I want? The question echoes in my head as I retake my position on stage. Professor Winters claps her hands, calling for everyone's attention, and I slip back into character.

But as rehearsal continues, I can't stop thinking about how David's fingers felt tangled in my hair, how his laugh rumbled against my chest when we were pressed together, how he'd look at me sometimes when he thought I was asleep.

I never wanted a relationship. That was our agreement—

no strings, no real names, no complications. Just physical connection whenever we both needed it.

So why does his absence feel like a gaping wound?

"YOU LOOK HOT," Quinn declares as I emerge from the bathroom in a fitted black dress and heeled boots. "Mike won't know what hit him."

I smooth down the fabric. "It's just drinks."

"It's just a fresh start," she corrects me, applying another layer of lip gloss. "Trust me, this is exactly what you need. A night out, cute guys, zero pressure."

I nod, trying to convince myself she's right. Life goes on. I can't keep dwelling on what happened. David clearly has no problem moving on—he hasn't texted, called, or made any attempt to contact me since Thanksgiving.

Not that I've reached out either. *What would I even say?* "Hey, funny how we've been fucking for months under fake names and turns out you're my best friend's brother! Want to grab coffee?"

The thought makes me laugh bitterly.

"What's funny?" Quinn asks, checking her reflection one last time.

"Nothing," I say quickly. "Just thinking about something from rehearsal."

Quinn grabs her purse and keys. "Ready to go?"

I nod, following her out the door. It's strange how you can miss someone you never really had. How you can yearn for something you deliberately avoided. My body remembers David's touch, craves it in a way I never experienced with previous hookups.

But what's done is done. Tonight, I'll smile and flirt with Mike. I'll drink just enough to forget the ache in my chest. I'll laugh at jokes and dance if asked. I'll be Whitney Barnes, drama student with big dreams, not Nikki who melted under Jax's hands in the darkness of his apartment.

Life goes on. It has to.

But as we walk to the bar, my phone stays heavy in my pocket, silent as it has been for two weeks straight, and I realize I've become that girl—the one waiting for a text that will never come.

McCaffrey's is packed tonight, the usual Thursday crowd spilling from booths onto the dance floor. The familiar scent of beer and cheap cologne hangs heavy in the air, mingling with the persistent bass thump that vibrates through my chest. Quinn's waving frantically at Mike and Tyler, who've already snagged a booth in the corner.

"Found you!" Quinn shouts over "Make You Mine," grabbing my hand and tugging me through the crowd.

I slide into the booth across from Tyler, and Mike immediately shifts closer to me, his cologne enveloping me in a cloud of something expensive and woodsy. Under different circumstances, I might appreciate his attention, the way his shoulders fill out his button-down shirt, his perfect white smile.

"You look amazing," he says, his eyes drifting appreciatively over my dress.

"Thanks." I tuck a curl behind my ear. "You clean up pretty well yourself."

Our server appears—a tired-looking girl with a septum piercing who's probably one of us, trying to pay tuition. "What can I get you guys?"

"Jack and Coke," Mike says confidently, showing his ID. Tyler orders a beer.

Quinn puts on her innocent sorority girl voice. "Diet Coke for me."

"Ginger ale," I add, sliding my fake ID back into my wallet. No need to use it here—the bartenders know the drill. Order something non-alcoholic, then have your legal friends buy shots later.

"So how was rehearsal?" Mike leans closer, his arm stretching across the back of the booth behind me. "You were pretty intense up there."

"It was good," I reply, consciously reminding myself to be present, to engage. "Opening night's in two weeks. Still have a few scenes to nail down."

"I bet you nail everything you try," he says, his voice dropping lower.

Quinn kicks me under the table, her eyes wide with encouragement.

I laugh, surprising myself with how genuine it sounds. "That was terrible."

Mike grins, not offended in the slightest. "Made you laugh, though."

"Fair point."

The drinks arrive, and Mike raises his glass. "To new beginnings."

The sentiment feels pointed, like Quinn told him exactly what I need to hear. I clink my glass against his anyway. "New beginnings."

The ginger ale is flat and overly sweet, but I sip it slowly, trying to keep the conversation flowing. Mike tells me about their last game, how they're heading to championships if they win against State next week. He's charming in a straightforward way—no games, no hidden agenda. He says what he means and means what he says. It's refreshing.

And nothing like David.

Stop. Don't go there.

Quinn and Tyler have drifted into their own private bubble. Her hand is on his thigh, his fingers playing with her hair as they whisper to each other. Every few minutes, Quinn laughs too loudly at something that probably isn't that funny.

"Want something stronger?" Mike asks, nodding toward my nearly empty glass.

"God, yes."

He returns from the bar with two tequila shots. The lime and salt ritual gives me something to do with my hands, something to focus on besides the gnawing emptiness I've been carrying around. The tequila burns a path down my throat, warming me from the inside.

"That's better," I say, and Mike grins.

"Another round?"

"Maybe in a minute." I lean back, studying him. "So why theatre? Don't tell me you're secretly into Shakespeare."

"I'm into talented, beautiful women," he answers immediately. "And I heard you were both."

The directness makes me laugh again. "You're really not subtle, are you?"

"Life's too short for subtlety." His knee brushes against mine under the table. "I've wanted to ask you out since Freshman Orientation when you read that monologue from—what was it? Something about a woman scorned?"

"Medea," I supply, genuinely surprised. "You remember that?"

"Hard to forget. You were scary good." His hand finds mine on the table. "So why'd you keep avoiding my texts?"

The question catches me off guard. I've been so wrapped up in this thing with David that I barely registered other guys' interest. "I wasn't avoiding you specifically. Just been busy with the play."

"And now?"

"Now..." I meet his gaze, forcing myself to stay in this moment, with this attractive guy who's making it very clear he's into me. "Now I'm here."

His thumb traces circles on my palm. "I'm glad."

The tequila loosens something in me, or maybe it's just the relief of distraction. I find myself genuinely smiling at Mike's stories, leaning into his space when he speaks. He's easy to talk to. Uncomplicated.

Quinn and Tyler have moved past talking entirely. They're making out now, her hands in his hair, his grip tight on her waist. The sight would normally make me roll my eyes, but tonight I feel a twist of envy. Not because I want Tyler—but because Quinn allows herself these uncomplicated pleasures without overthinking everything.

"They're not exactly shy, are they?" Mike comments, watching them.

"Quinn doesn't do shy."

His focus returns to me, gaze dropping to my lips. "What about you?"

The question hangs between us, heavy with implication. This is the moment to decide—lean in or pull back.

"I'm selective," I reply, holding his gaze.

He smiles, moving closer. "Lucky me."

When his lips touch mine, I wait for the spark, that electric current I feel—felt—with David. Mike's kiss is nice. Confident. His lips are soft, his technique practiced. But it's like kissing a stranger, which, technically, he is.

So was David, once.

I pull back slightly, hoping my disappointment doesn't show. Mike's eyes are still closed, his expression pleased.

"I've been wanting to do that for a long time," he murmurs.

"Yeah?" I attempt to recapture the flirty mood from earlier. "Was it worth the wait?"

"Definitely." His hand cups my face. "Can I do it again?"

I nod, closing my eyes as he leans in. Maybe the second time will be better. Maybe I just need to give this a chance. His lips press against mine more firmly this time, his hand sliding into my hair.

I'm trying—really trying—to feel something, anything close to the desire that consumed me whenever David touched me. But there's nothing. Just the mechanical movement of lips against lips, the awareness of being kissed without the surrender.

I open my eyes mid-kiss, frustrated with myself, and that's when I see him.

David.

He's seated at the bar, his back to me, but I'd recognize that profile anywhere. The strong jawline, the way he runs his hand through his blonde hair when he's listening intently. My heart stutters painfully in my chest.

He's not alone.

A woman sits beside him, her curly hair cascading down her back, mixed-race caramel skin glowing under the bar lights. She's gorgeous—curvy in all the right places, laughing at something he's said. As I watch, frozen in my booth with Mike's lips still on mine, she places her hand on David's forearm, leaning closer.

The familiar ache I've been carrying for two weeks sharpens into something unbearable. It slices through me, stealing my breath, making my eyes sting with sudden tears.

Of course he moved on. Why wouldn't he? We were nothing to each other. Just bodies in the dark. Fake names and empty promises to call again soon.

I break the kiss abruptly, my lungs constricting.

"Whitney? You okay?" Mike's voice sounds far away, muffled by the roaring in my ears.

"Fine," I manage. "Just—need some air."

But I can't tear my eyes away from the bar. From David laughing with this beautiful stranger, looking exactly like he did with me, before everything fell apart. *Does she know his real name? Or is she another "Nikki" in his rotation of meaningless hookups?*

And why does that thought hurt so fucking much?

Quinn finally comes up for air, her lipstick smudged beyond repair. "Whit, you look like you've seen a ghost."

I have. The ghost of whatever I thought David and I might have been, if things had been different.

"I don't feel great," I say, the truth in more ways than one. "I think I should go."

Mike's hand finds mine under the table. "I can walk you back to your dorm."

"No," I say too quickly. "I mean, you guys stay. Enjoy yourselves. I just need some sleep."

Quinn frowns, finally following my gaze to the bar. She spots her brother immediately, her expression darkening. "Shit."

"It's fine," I insist, though it's anything but fine. "I'm fine."

"Whitney—"

"Really, Quinn." I force a smile. "I'm just tired from rehearsal. You stay. Have fun with Tyler." I turn to Mike. "Rain check?"

He looks disappointed but nods. "I'll text you?"

"Sure." I stand, grabbing my purse, desperate to escape before David turns around and sees me. Before I have to witness him flirting with another woman up close.

As I push through the crowded bar toward the exit, I feel hollow, like someone has scooped out everything inside me and left just enough to keep walking. Two weeks of silence, of wondering if he ever thinks of me, and here he is—already with someone new.

The cool night air hits my face as I step outside, bringing no relief from the burning behind my eyes. I'd told myself all along I didn't want more than what we had. That relationships were messy and complicated and not worth the inevitable heartbreak.

But standing here alone while David moves on without a second thought, I realize I've managed to get my heart broken anyway.

ELEVEN

No Personal Questions

DAVID HUNTER

I FIDDLE with the napkin under my drink, twisting it into a tight spiral while Amber—or was it Amanda?—runs her manicured fingernails along my forearm. The bar's too loud tonight, bass thumping through the floorboards of McCaffrey's like a second heartbeat. Every thud reminds me I've been a complete idiot these past two weeks.

"So anyway," she continues, batting mascara-heavy lashes at me, "that's when I told my professor he could take his opinion and shove it where the sun don't shine."

I force a laugh that sounds hollow even to my own ears. "Ballsy move."

"I know, right?" She leans in closer, her perfume sweet

but overwhelming. "I've always been the type to speak my mind."

I nod, pretending to be captivated while my attention drifts toward the door for the fifteenth time in twenty minutes. I shouldn't be here. Should've stayed at my apartment, buried myself in equations and problem sets instead of marinating in whiskey at the campus watering hole.

The bartender slides another Jack and Coke my way. I didn't even order it, but Jimmy knows my routine by now. Three drinks in and I'm usually chatting up the prettiest girl at the bar. Tonight's candidate is right beside me, hanging on my every half-assed word.

"You're really quiet tonight," she says, twirling a strand of her curly hair. "Not that I mind the mysterious type."

"Sorry, just got a lot on my mind. Finals coming up."

It's not entirely a lie. I do have finals. But they're not what's got me twisted inside out like a damn pretzel. No, that honor belongs to—

The air in the room shifts.

I don't need to turn around to know she's here. It's like my body has developed some kind of Whitney Barnes radar. My shoulders tense, neck prickling with awareness before I even catch sight of her.

When I do finally look, I wish I hadn't.

Whitney's sliding into a booth on the far side of the bar, her sleek black dress hugging curves I know all too well. Her short curls frame her face perfectly, that face that's been haunting me since Thanksgiving. But she's not alone.

Mike fucking Williams is right beside her, his arm draped around her shoulder like he owns her. The wide receiver's varsity jacket might as well be a neon sign announcing his status on campus.

"Shit," I mutter, turning back to face the bar so fast I nearly knock over my drink.

"Something wrong?" Amber-Amanda asks, her hand now resting on my thigh.

"Nothing. Just saw someone I know." I drain my glass in one burning gulp, signaling Jimmy for another. "Make it a double."

The bartender raises an eyebrow but doesn't comment. When he returns with my drink, I down half of it immediately, welcoming the fire that spreads through my chest. Better than the ice forming there as I picture Whitney with Williams.

"So," I say, suddenly focused entirely on my companion, "tell me more about yourself."

"Well," she brightens, clearly pleased by my renewed interest, "I'm double-majoring in Communications and African American Studies. I'm hoping to work in media representation after graduation."

I lean closer, forcing myself to pay attention. She's beautiful—mixed-race with honey-colored skin and eyes that tilt upward at the corners. The kind of girl who normally would have my full attention without me having to try.

"That's impressive," I say, and mean it. "Takes dedication to handle two majors."

"I'm nothing if not dedicated." Her smile turns suggestive. "When I want something, I go after it."

I can't help glancing back over my shoulder. Whitney's laughing at something Williams said, her head tilted back exposing the line of her throat. I know exactly how that skin feels beneath my lips.

My stomach clenches. What the actual hell is wrong

with me? This isn't who I am. David "Jax" Hunter doesn't pine after hookups.

"You keep looking over there," Amber or Amanda says, annoyance creeping into her tone. "Ex-girlfriend or something?"

"Nothing like that. Just someone I used to know." I turn back to her, summoning my most charming smile. "Sorry, where were we?"

"You were about to tell me why a hot engineering major is sitting alone at a bar on a Friday night."

I laugh, feeling my shoulders loosen slightly. "Well, I wouldn't say alone. I've got good company now, don't I?"

"Smooth," she says, rolling her eyes but smiling. "I'm Alyssa, by the way."

Damn. Not even close.

"David," I reply, extending my hand formally like we're at a business meeting instead of a bar. She takes it, holding on a beat longer than necessary.

"So David, what's your story?"

I open my mouth to deliver my standard lines—the ones that usually lead to a night of no-strings fun—when a burst of laughter from Whitney's table cuts through the music. My gaze betrays me again, drawn to her like a magnet.

Williams is kissing her neck now, and Whitney's eyes are closed, a small smile playing on her lips. The same lips that pressed against mine countless times over the past few months.

"Fuck this," I mutter, grabbing my drink and draining it.

"Excuse me?" Alyssa looks startled.

"Sorry, not you." I shake my head. "Just remembered something I need to take care of."

I signal Jimmy for another shot. He delivers, along with a concerned look. "Slowing down anytime soon, Hunter?"

"Night's just getting started, Jim." I swallow the shot in one go, grimacing at the burn.

Alyssa places her hand on mine. "You know, whatever's bothering you, alcohol's just a temporary fix."

"That's all I need. Temporary." I flash her a grin that doesn't reach my eyes. "Just like everything else in life, right?"

She studies me for a moment. "You don't mean that."

"Don't I?" I laugh without humor. "Show me one thing that lasts."

"My parents have been married forty years," she says simply.

That shuts me up. I think about my own parents—my mom stuck in a loveless marriage for financial security, my dad who's more married to his work than his wife. What a joke.

"Lucky them," I say finally. "Outliers in the data set."

Another round arrives unbidden. Jimmy's starting to look concerned, but he knows I tip well.

I feel Whitney's presence like a physical weight. Even without looking, I know exactly where she is in the room. It's maddening.

"You know what?" I turn fully toward Alyssa, deliberately positioning myself so Whitney's out of my line of sight. "Tell me more about your studies."

Alyssa's entire face lights up, and guilt gnaws at me. She deserves better than being a distraction from my Whitney problem.

"Actually, I'm researching how mixed-race representation

in media affects identity formation," she says, leaning forward. "It's fascinating stuff."

"I bet," I say, genuinely interested despite myself. "Must be personal for you too."

"Exactly! That's why—"

A familiar laugh cuts through the noise again. My jaw clenches involuntarily.

"That's it." Alyssa stands abruptly, grabbing her purse. "I'm not going to sit here while you moon over whoever that is. I have finals to study for anyway."

"Wait—" I start, but know I have no right to ask her to stay.

"Good luck with whatever this is," she gestures vaguely at me before walking away.

Great. Just fucking perfect.

I spin my empty glass on the counter, debating whether to order another or just call it a night. The mature move would be to leave, but maturity's never been my strong suit.

I wave for another drink, and as I wait, I make the mistake of looking over at Whitney's booth again.

This time, she's full-on making out with Williams. His massive hand cradles the back of her head, fingers threading through those curls I've touched so many times. Something dark and possessive surges through me, an emotion I've never allowed myself to feel before.

"Shit," I mutter, grabbing my fresh drink and turning away.

A redhead at the other end of the bar catches my eye and smiles. Under normal circumstances, I'd be over there in a heartbeat, working my charm. Instead, I lift my glass in acknowledgment but stay put.

The truth hits me like a freight train: I'm jealous. Stupidly, irrationally jealous over a woman I never even called my girlfriend. A woman who knows me as "Jax," not David. A woman who is my sister's roommate, for fuck's sake.

I drain half my drink, letting the alcohol blur the edges of my thoughts. What was our rule again? No personal questions. No real names. No attachments.

Clearly, I've broken that last one without even realizing it.

The music changes to something slower, more sultry. Couples gravitate toward each other all around the bar. I check my phone—barely past midnight. The night stretches endlessly ahead of me.

One more glance. I can't help myself.

Whitney's alone at the booth now, Williams nowhere in sight. She's staring into her drink, looking almost... sad? No, that can't be right. My alcohol-addled brain is seeing what it wants to see.

Jimmy refills my water glass without me asking. "Might want to switch to this for a while, Hunter."

"Since when are you my mother?" I grumble, but drink the water anyway.

I slump against the bar counter, staring at the melting ice in my watered-down whiskey. Another girl slides onto the stool next to me—brunette, killer smile, legs for days—but I barely glance her way. She tries the usual opener, something about having seen me in one of her engineering electives, but I give her nothing more than a distracted nod.

"Not feeling too social?" she asks, undeterred.

"Not tonight."

She waits a beat, then shrugs. "Your loss," she says,

already sliding off the stool to find more promising territory.

Under normal circumstances, I'd have kicked myself for letting that opportunity walk away. Tonight, I couldn't care less. The brunette disappears into the crowd, and my eyes drift back to Whitney's booth.

Empty.

I sit up straight, scanning the bar. Williams is over by the pool tables, laughing with his teammates, a beer in his massive paw of a hand—but no Whitney. *Where'd she go?* My eyes dart around the crowded space, heart rate accelerating like I've just downed three Red Bulls.

Maybe the bathroom? I glance toward the hallway leading to the restrooms.

Before I can think better of it, I'm sliding off my stool, the room tilting slightly as my feet hit the floor. *Shit, I'm drunker than I thought.* I steady myself against the bar for a second, then weave through the crowd toward the bathrooms.

The logical part of my brain—what's left of it, anyway—is screaming that this is a terrible idea. *What am I planning to do? Ambush her outside the ladies' room?* Demand to know why she's sucking face with Williams when just weeks ago she was in my bed? I sound like a jealous boyfriend, which is exactly what I've spent years avoiding becoming.

Yet I can't stop myself from moving forward, each step fueled by alcohol and something that feels dangerously like heartbreak.

I'm almost to the hallway when a solid mass plants itself in my path. Two hands grip my shoulders firmly, stopping me in my tracks.

"What do you think you're doing?"

I blink, struggling to focus on the face in front of me. Blonde hair. Green eyes narrowed in suspicion. A face that looks irritatingly similar to my own.

"Quinn?" I slur, confused. "The hell are you doing here?"

My sister tightens her grip on my shoulders, steering me away from the bathrooms and toward a quieter corner. "I'm here with Tyler … and Whitney and Mike." She eyes me up and down, frowning. "Jesus, Davey, how much have you had to drink?"

"Not enough," I mutter, attempting to sidestep her. "Need to talk to Whitney."

Quinn blocks my path again. "Yeah, that's not happening. Not in this state."

"Is she in the bathroom?"

My sister rolls her eyes. "No, genius. She just left."

The words hit me like a bucket of ice water. "Left? With Williams?"

"No." Quinn studies my face, her expression softening slightly. "Alone, actually. She said she had a headache and was heading home."

"So Williams struck out?" I can't keep the hopeful note from my voice.

Quinn narrows her eyes. "What's it to you? You haven't spoken to her since Thanksgiving."

"That's not—" I start to protest, then cut myself off. It's true. I haven't texted, called, nothing. Just spent two weeks drowning in schoolwork and pretending I wasn't thinking about her constantly. "I was giving her space."

"Space," Quinn repeats flatly. "Right."

I run a hand through my hair, frustration mounting. "You don't understand."

"Actually, I understand perfectly." Quinn crosses her arms. "You're doing what you always do—running away the moment things get complicated. The David Hunter special."

Her words sting because they're true. I lean against the wall, suddenly exhausted. "It's not that simple."

"It never is with you." She sighs, then shakes her head. "Look, if you genuinely care about Whitney, which your pathetic drunk ass seems to suggest, she just left. Like, two minutes ago. If you hurry, you might catch her before she gets a ride."

My heart lurches. "She's outside?"

"Probably waiting for her Uber by the front entrance. But Davey—" Quinn grabs my arm as I start to move, her expression serious. "Don't play with her. She's not just another conquest. She's my friend, and she's been through enough."

I want to defend myself, to explain that Whitney was never just a conquest, but there's no time. I nod instead. "Got it."

"And for God's sake, text me when you get home so I know you didn't wrap your car around a tree."

"Yes, mom," I mutter, already pulling away.

"You're welcome, asshole!" she calls after me.

I weave through the packed bar, bumping shoulders and mumbling half-hearted apologies. The alcohol makes everything hazy around the edges, but my purpose is crystal clear: find Whitney. The crowd parts just enough for me to spot the exit, and I push forward with renewed determination.

As I near the door, doubt creeps in. *What the hell am I doing? What am I going to say to her? Sorry I've been ghosting you since discovering you're my sister's roommate? Sorry I saw you kissing Williams and lost my mind with jealousy?*

Maybe this is a mistake. Maybe I should just go home, sleep it off, and pretend none of this ever happened. Go back to being David Hunter, the guy who keeps it casual. The guy who doesn't get hurt because he never lets anyone close enough to hurt him.

I pause at the door, one hand on the handle.

A flash of memory hits me—Whitney's laugh as I told her some stupid joke. The way she curled against me afterward, neither of us speaking but neither rushing to leave either. How she'd trace patterns on my chest, lost in thought.

Before I can second-guess myself further, I push through the door into the cold December air.

The temperature change is jarring, sobriety slapping me across the face. Students cluster in small groups outside the bar, cigarette smoke and laughter mingling in the frosty air. I scan the sidewalk desperately, looking for her familiar silhouette.

And there she is.

Whitney stands alone at the edge of the curb, arms wrapped around herself against the cold, staring down at her phone. The yellow glow of the streetlight catches in her curls, illuminating her profile. Even from here, I can see her breath forming small clouds in the night air.

She looks up, as if sensing my presence, and our eyes lock across the distance. Something flickers across her face—surprise, maybe confusion. For one endless moment, neither of us moves.

Then her phone lights up, and she breaks our connection to glance down at it. A car pulls up—her ride.

It's now or never.

I step forward, my heart pounding in my ears louder than the bass from the bar behind me. I have no idea what I'm going to say, what I want from her, what any of this means. I just know I can't let her leave.

Not again. Not without trying.

Whitney looks back up, hesitating with her hand on the car door. Her eyes find mine again, questioning, waiting.

I take another step toward her.

"Stay the night with me?"

TWELVE

Real Names Only

DAVID HUNTER

I'M FUMBLING with my keys at the apartment door, a familiar routine made impossibly difficult by the five shots of whiskey swimming through my bloodstream. Whitney stands behind me, arms crossed, radiating a cold fury I can feel against my back.

Whitney brushes past me, the scent of her perfume—vanilla and something floral—momentarily disarming me. It's the same scent that lingered on my sheets for days after our last hookup. Before everything got complicated. Before I knew she was my sister's best friend. Before I saw her with that football asshole.

I flip on the lights and toss my keys onto the counter. My apartment looks exactly like I left it this morning—half-empty coffee mug on the table, engineering textbooks spread across the couch, dirty dishes in the sink. Not exactly the romantic setting for whatever this confrontation is about to become.

I watch Whitney through a whiskey-hazed blur as she moves around my apartment with practiced ease. She knows exactly where to hang her coat, which drawer holds the take-out menus, how to adjust the temperamental thermostat that's always either too hot or too cold. Never just right. Kind of like us.

"So," I clear my throat, trying to sound more sober than I feel. "I'm guessing this isn't a booty call."

Whitney turns to face me, her short black curls framing her face in a way that makes my chest tighten. "We need to talk, David."

"*Now* she uses my real name." The words come out harsher than intended, but the image of her lips pressed against Mike Williams' keeps flashing in my mind like a neon sign. "That's progress."

"Don't be an ass." She kicks off her shoes and curls up in the corner of my couch, moving my textbooks aside without a second thought. How many nights has she spent exactly there, her head on my shoulder, some mindless show playing on TV while we pretended we weren't counting the minutes until we could tear each other's clothes off?

I grab a glass of water from the kitchen, desperate to clear my head. When I return, Whitney's examining the spine of my fluid dynamics textbook with a vague interest that I know is just stalling.

"How drunk are you right now?" she asks without looking up.

"Drunk enough to tell the truth. Sober enough to remember it tomorrow." I sit on the opposite end of the couch, maintaining distance that feels both necessary and unbearable. "What do you want to talk about, Whitney? Or should I still call you Nikki?"

Her eyes flash. "You know that's not fair."

"Fair?" I laugh, but there's no humor in it. "You know what's not fair? Finding out the girl I've been sleeping with for months is my sister's roommate. Or watching her make out with some football player at McCaffrey's like what we had meant nothing."

"What we had?" Whitney stands up now, pacing the small space between the couch and TV. "We had sex, David. That's what you wanted, remember? That was our whole arrangement."

She's right, and that makes me angrier. "So if it was just sex, why are you here?"

"I don't know." Her voice softens, vulnerability sneaking in between her words. "I just... I couldn't stop thinking about Thanksgiving. About your face when you saw me in your parents' living room."

The memory hits me like a physical blow. My sister's roommate. The girl I'd been fantasizing about for months was my sister's fucking roommate. The cosmic joke of it all still makes me want to punch something.

"Yeah, well." I run a hand through my hair, feeling the alcohol make my movements clumsy. "That was a real sitcom moment."

Whitney sits back down, closer this time. I can see the rise and fall of her chest, the way her fingers twist nervously in her lap. "Quinn's still pissed at both of us."

"Quinn will get over it." I'm not actually sure about that. My sister has been sending me one-word texts for two weeks. "She's just freaked out that her roommate and her brother were—"

"Fucking?" Whitney supplies, her eyes meeting mine with a challenge.

The word hangs between us, loaded with memories. Her body underneath mine. The way she'd grab my shoulders, hard enough to leave marks. The sound of her laugh afterward, when we'd lie tangled in sheets, pretending we weren't counting down to when one of us would make an excuse to leave.

"Yeah." My mouth feels dry. "That."

Whitney looks around my apartment, her gaze lingering on the kitchen where we once couldn't even make it to the bedroom, the hallway where I'd pinned her against the wall more times than I can count, the bathroom door that's still slightly crooked from when we slammed into it.

"I've spent so much time here," she says quietly. "But I never knew I was in David Hunter's apartment. I thought I was with Jax, some marketing student I matched with who didn't want strings attached."

"And I thought I was with Nikki, some business student who was too focused on her career to want a boyfriend." I feel my defenses rising again. "Seems like we both got what we wanted."

"Did we?" Her question catches me off guard. "Because I'm here, aren't you? And you let me in, even though you're clearly pissed at me."

She's not wrong. She agreed to come to my apartment. But something pulled me toward her, the same gravity that's always existed between us.

"I'm not pissed at you," I lie, then immediately correct myself. "Okay, I am. But not because of the fake name thing. That was mutual deception."

"Then why are you so angry?"

The whiskey makes me brave. Or stupid. Probably both. I lean against the counter, trying to look casual despite the room's slight spinning. "You could've stayed with your boyfriend."

"Mike is not my boyfriend."

"Could've fooled me. You two seemed pretty cozy with your tongue down his throat."

Whitney's eyes narrow. "That's rich coming from you. Who was that girl you were all over at the bar? The one hanging on your every word like you're some kind of god?"

"I don't even know her name." The admission sounds pathetic even to my ears.

"Wow. That makes it so much better."

I run a hand through my hair, frustration building. "What do you want from me, Whitney? You made it clear at Thanksgiving that what we had was nothing. Just a hookup, right? 'Nikki' and 'Jax' meeting up for casual sex whenever the mood struck."

"That was our agreement!" Her voice rises. "No complications. No strings. Just fun."

"Then why are you here? Why'd you leave with me instead of staying with Mike?"

She throws her hands up. "I don't know! Maybe because you looked so pathetic sitting there trying to drink yourself stupid."

The words sting more than they should. "I wasn't pathetic."

"You ordered six shots in twenty minutes, David. You were on your way to alcohol poisoning."

"I was fine."

"You were jealous."

The accusation hangs between us. I want to deny it, but the liquor in my system has dismantled my filter. "And what if I was?"

Whitney steps back, surprise flickering across her face. "You don't get to be jealous. That's not what we agreed to."

"We didn't agree to anything!" I push off from the counter, closing the distance between us. "We met on a dating app using fake names. We fucked a few times. Then I find out you're my sister's best friend, and suddenly everything is complicated."

"It's only complicated because you're making it complicated!"

"No, it's complicated because I can't stop thinking about you!" The words escape before I can catch them. "It's complicated because everything changed when I found out who you really are. It's complicated because seeing you with that meathead tonight made me want to punch something."

Whitney's eyes widen, her chest rising and falling with quick breaths. "You don't own me."

"I know that."

"We're not in a relationship."

"I know."

"Then why are you acting like a jealous boyfriend?"

The question stops me short. She's right. I have no claim on her, no right to feel this burning in my chest when I think about her with someone else. I'm acting like the exact kind of man I swore I'd never become—possessive, emotional, vulnerable.

I turn away, bracing myself against the kitchen counter. "You're right. This is stupid. I'm drunk and saying stupid things."

The silence that follows stretches for so long I wonder if she's left. Then I feel her hand on my shoulder.

"I saw you with that girl, and I hated it." Her voice is soft, almost a whisper. "I have no right to hate it, but I did."

I turn to face her, finding her closer than I expected. "Why?"

"I don't know." She shakes her head, those short black curls framing her face in a way that makes my fingers itch to touch them. "Maybe for the same reason you hated seeing me with Mike."

We stare at each other, the electricity that's always been there between us crackling with new intensity. I'm acutely aware of every detail—the small mole just below her left ear, the slight smudge of her eyeliner, the pulse visible at the base of her throat.

"This wasn't supposed to happen," I say, my voice hoarse.

"What wasn't?"

"Feelings."

Whitney laughs, but it sounds brittle. "We don't have feelings. We have chemistry."

"Is that what you call it? Because I've had chemistry with other women before, and it never felt like this."

"Like what?"

"Like I'm going insane when I'm not with you." I step closer, emboldened by the alcohol and the vulnerability in her eyes. "Like I can't think straight when you're around. Like I'm jealous of anyone who gets to touch you who isn't me."

Her breath catches. "David…"

"Tell me I'm wrong. Tell me you don't feel it too."

She doesn't answer with words. Instead, she grabs the front of my shirt and pulls me toward her, our lips crashing together with a force that feels like inevitability.

I press her against the wall, my hands finding her waist, her skin hot even through the fabric of her dress. She tastes like vodka cranberry and desire, her tongue darting against mine with a hunger that matches my own. One of her legs hooks around mine, drawing me closer until we're pressed together with nothing but clothing between us.

"This doesn't change anything," she gasps between kisses, her fingers already working on the buttons of my shirt.

"Absolutely not," I agree, tracing the line of her jaw with my lips, down to that spot on her neck that I know drives her wild. She moans, her head falling back against the wall. "Still no complications."

"None." Her hands push my shirt off my shoulders, her nails dragging lightly down my chest. "Just chemistry."

"Just chemistry," I echo, finding the zipper of her dress and pulling it down in one smooth motion.

The dress pools at her feet, leaving her in nothing but a black lace bra and matching panties. The sight of her nearly undoes me—smooth brown skin, soft curves, the heat in her eyes that tells me she wants this as badly as I do.

I lift her, her legs wrapping around my waist, carrying her toward my bedroom. Every step is torture, her body pressed against mine, her mouth hot on my neck, marking me in ways I know I'll see tomorrow.

We fall onto my bed in a tangle of limbs and half-removed clothing. There's a desperation to our movements that wasn't there before—a need that goes beyond physical release. I take my time with her, tracing every curve, every dip and hollow of her body with my hands and mouth.

"David," she breathes, and hearing my real name on her lips as she arches beneath me sends fire racing through my veins.

"Say it again," I demand, my voice rough with desire.

"David." Her fingers dig into my shoulders, pulling me closer. "Please."

I enter her slowly, watching her face as her eyes flutter closed and her lips part on a moan. It's different this time—deeper, more intense. Every thrust feels like confession, every touch like a promise neither of us is ready to make.

Whitney's eyes open, locking with mine as we move together, the connection almost too intense to bear. There's something in her gaze I've never seen before—vulnerability, trust, something dangerously close to the feelings we've both been denying.

"Don't stop," she whispers, and I'm not sure if she means the sex or whatever else is happening between us in this moment.

I kiss her deeply as we both come undone, swallowing her cries, and feeling her body tense and release around mine. For a moment, everything else disappears—the complications, the arguments, the jealousy. There's just Whitney and me, tangled together in the dark, breathing hard, holding on to something neither of us can name.

In the quiet aftermath, her head on my chest, my fingers tracing lazy patterns on her bare shoulder, neither of us speaks. The words hang unspoken between us: this is more than chemistry. This is more than casual. This is something we never planned for.

THIRTEEN

Whatever This Is

WHITNEY BARNES

WARM LIGHT STREAMS through David's blinds, painting golden stripes across our entangled bodies. My eyes flutter open, adjusting to the daylight that exposes what darkness usually conceals. I'm in David's—not Jax's—arms, and something feels different. The anonymity of night is gone, replaced by an honesty that terrifies me.

His chest rises and falls against my back, his breath warming my neck. I've never stayed until daylight before. Our arrangement has always been simple: meet, hook up, leave before things get complicated. But last night ripped our rulebook to shreds.

The clock on his nightstand reads 1:22 PM. I've been here all night and half the day, wrapped in his sheets, his scent, his world.

"Morning, beautiful," David murmurs, voice still thick with sleep. His lips brush against my shoulder, and I feel that familiar fire ignite. But there's something else now—a warmth that goes deeper than desire.

I turn to face him, pulling the sheet around my naked body. "It's afternoon, actually."

"Is it?" He smiles, and my heart does this stupid little dance I'm not prepared for. "I've never seen you in the daylight like this. You're even prettier than I remembered."

His fingers trace my jawline, and I fight the urge to lean into his touch. "Stop flattering me." I try to sound casual, but my voice betrays me.

"Flattery would imply I'm exaggerating." His eyes hold mine, no longer hidden beneath the mask of darkness or our fake identities. "I'm just stating facts, Whitney."

My name on his lips shoots electricity down my spine. Not Nikki—Whitney. The real me.

"This is weird, right?" I ask, studying the contours of his face—the sharp jawline, the slight stubble, those hazel eyes that somehow look greener in the daylight. "Being here like this. Together. Knowing who we really are."

David props himself up on one elbow, the sheet sliding down to reveal his bare chest. "Weird? Maybe. But also... I don't know. Nice?"

"Nice?" I let out a laugh that's too breathy to be casual. "That's what you're going with?"

"Better than nice. Amazing. Unexpected. A little frightening." His honesty disarms me. "I never thought I'd want someone to stay until morning, let alone into the afternoon. But with you..."

I press my palm against his chest, feeling his heartbeat quicken. "Quinn will kill us both."

"Quinn doesn't get a vote in this." His hand slides over mine, holding it against his heart. "Whatever this is."

"And what is this?" I ask, finally voicing the question that's been hanging between us.

Instead of answering, David leans forward and kisses me. It's different from our previous kisses—slower, more deliberate. There's no rush to get to the main event. This kiss is the event itself.

When he pulls away, his eyes are darker. "I don't have labels for it yet. I just know I want to keep kissing you."

His hands slide beneath the sheet, finding my breasts. His touch is reverent, almost worshipful. "God, you're perfect."

I arch into his hands, my body responding automatically to his touch. "Acting school," I quip, trying to diffuse the intensity with humor. "It's all about body control."

David laughs, his thumb circling my nipple. "Is that what they teach you? Because I'd like to enroll immediately."

"Sorry, you need talent to get in." I bite my lip as his mouth replaces his fingers, his tongue teasing my sensitive skin.

"I'm talented," he murmurs against my breast. "Very, *very* talented."

He proves his point by taking my nipple between his lips, sucking gently at first, then with increasing pressure that sends waves of pleasure through my body.

"David," I breathe, tangling my fingers in his hair.

"I love hearing my real name on your lips," he says, moving to my other breast. "Say it again."

"David." It comes out as a moan this time.

His hands continue their exploration, mapping my body with agonizing slowness. We've had sex before—hot, intense, mind-blowing sex—but this feels like the first time he's truly seen me.

"You're driving me crazy," I whisper as his tongue traces circles around my nipple.

"That's the plan." He looks up at me with a wicked grin.

Something shifts in me. I'm tired of being passive. With a swift movement, I push him onto his back and straddle him, the sheet falling away completely now.

"My turn," I say, leaning down to kiss him.

His hands find my hips, but I catch his wrists and pin them above his head. "No touching. Not yet."

David's eyes widen, then darken with desire. "Yes, ma'am."

I roll my hips against his, feeling him hard beneath me. The power I have over him in this moment is intoxicating. I release his hands and sit up straight, giving him a full view of my naked body.

"You know what the difference is between now and before?" I ask, slowly grinding against him without letting him inside.

He swallows hard. "What?"

"Before, we were strangers pretending to know each other's bodies." I lean down, my breasts brushing against his chest. "Now we're just starting to learn who we really are."

I capture his mouth in a kiss, teasing him with my tongue the way I'm teasing him with my body. His hands move to my hips again, and this time I let him, enjoying the way his fingers dig into my skin.

"Whitney," he groans as I position myself above him, letting just the tip of him enter me before pulling away.

"Patience," I whisper, enjoying the tortured look on his face.

I continue my teasing, giving him just enough to make him crazy before taking it away. His hands slide up to cup my breasts, thumbs flicking over my nipples in a way that makes me lose my rhythm momentarily.

"Two can play at this game," he says with a victorious smirk.

The tension between us builds until I can't stand it anymore. I need him inside me. But as I position myself to take him fully, I make the mistake of looking directly into his eyes.

Time seems to stop. Those hazel eyes, greener now in the afternoon light, stare back at me with an expression I've never seen before. Not lust—though that's there too—but something deeper. Something that makes my chest tight and my throat close up.

In that moment, the truth hits me like a physical blow: I'm in love with him.

The realization sends panic coursing through my veins. I love him. I love David Hunter. The one thing I swore I'd never do—fall for someone when my career is just taking off—and I've done it anyway.

"Whitney?" David's voice breaks through my spiral. "You okay?"

I scramble off him, suddenly desperate for distance. "I need to go."

Confusion clouds his features. "What? Why?"

"I just—I need to get home." I search frantically for my clothes, finding my underwear tangled in the sheets.

David sits up, concern replacing desire. "Did I do something wrong?"

"No, it's not you." I pull on my panties, then spot my

bra draped over his desk chair. "I remembered I have a line reading with Quinn this afternoon."

"On a Saturday?" His skepticism is clear. "Whitney, talk to me."

"There's nothing to talk about." I hook my bra and search for my jeans. "This was fun, but I really need to go."

He catches my wrist as I reach for my shirt. "Don't do this. Don't run away."

I pull free from his grasp. "I'm not running away. I have commitments."

"Bullshit." He stands now, gloriously naked and unashamed. "Something just happened. I saw it in your eyes."

"Nothing happened." I yank my shirt over my head, avoiding his gaze. "We had fun, like always."

"This wasn't like always, and you know it." His voice softens. "Whatever you're thinking, whatever you're feeling—I probably feel it too."

My heart stutters. That's exactly what I'm afraid of.

"I can't do this right now." I finally find my jeans and

pull them on. "I have auditions coming up. The showcase is in two weeks. I need to focus."

"So focus. I'm not asking you to choose."

"Aren't you?" I challenge, finally meeting his eyes. "Relationships take time, energy, commitment. I don't have any of that to spare right now."

"Who said anything about a relationship?" But his eyes tell a different story.

"Nobody had to say it." My hands shake as I button my jeans. "It's what happens next. We keep seeing each other, we fall deeper, and suddenly I'm making choices based on us instead of my career."

David runs a hand through his hair, frustration evident. "That's not fair. You don't know what I want or expect."

"I know what I can give, and right now, it's not much." I grab my phone from his nightstand, checking the time. "I really do need to go."

"So that's it?" His voice hardens. "One moment of real connection and you're out the fuckin' door?"

I pause, my hand on the doorknob. Was I already in love with him before today? Has it been building all along, disguised as lust and chemistry? The thought terrifies me even more.

"I gotta go." My voice comes out steadier than I feel.

He stares at me for a moment, my hand on the door. "Then go."

Satin sheets are very romantic, what happens when you're not in bed?

I practically fly down the stairs of David's apartment building, my breath coming in short gasps that have nothing to do with physical exertion. My hands shake as I pull out my phone to call an Uber, nearly dropping it on the concrete sidewalk. I can't be here when—if—he comes after me.

Three minutes. The app says three minutes until my ride arrives.

I walk to the corner, putting more distance between myself and David's building, between myself and whatever just happened up there. The afternoon air feels sharp against my skin, or maybe that's just the adrenaline making everything feel more intense.

"What happens when you're not in bed?" The lyric from an old Madonna song floats through my mind uninvited.

My mama used to blast that song on Saturday mornings while cleaning the house, singing along as she dusted and vacuumed. I never really understood what it meant until *now*.

Because what *does* happen when you're not in bed? When the physical connection fades and you're left with... feelings?

I wrap my arms around myself, suddenly cold despite the mild temperature. This pain in my chest, this tightness that makes it hard to breathe—is this what love feels like? If so, how do people voluntarily sign up for this torture?

A memory flashes: David's face this morning, soft with sleep, looking at me like I was something precious. Not just a body to satisfy his needs, but a person he wanted to know. To keep.

My throat tightens. I've spent years building walls around my heart, focusing on my career, my ambitions. One morning in the daylight with David, and those walls crumble like they were made of sand.

I glance back at his building, half-expecting—half-hoping—to see him running after me. The entrance remains empty.

Love isn't supposed to hurt like this. It's supposed to be beautiful, supportive. This feeling is like having my skin peeled away, leaving everything raw and exposed. I'm terrified of what would happen if I stayed—if I admitted to myself—to him—what I'm feeling.

What if he doesn't feel the same? What if he does?

Both possibilities terrify me equally.

A blue Honda pulls up to the curb, and I check the license plate against my app. My Uber.

"Whitney?" the driver calls through the open window.

"Yes." My voice sounds strange to my own ears, like it belongs to someone else.

As I slide into the backseat, I look down at my phone. The screen remains stubbornly blank. No texts. No calls. Nothing.

Did I expect David to text, begging me to come back? To fight for whatever was happening between us? A part of me did, I realize with a sinking feeling. But there's nothing.

The car pulls away from the curb, and I watch David's apartment building recede in the rear window. *Maybe this is for the best. Clean breaks heal faster, right?*

But if that's true, why does it feel like my heart is being torn in half?

"You okay back there?" The driver's eyes meet mine in the rearview mirror.

"I'm fine." The lie comes automatically.

We drive in silence, the city passing by in a blur outside my window. I keep checking my phone, willing it to light up with David's name. But it remains dark, and with each passing minute, the reality sinks in deeper.

We're over. For real this time.

Not "Jax and Nikki"—they never really existed. David and Whitney—whatever we might have become—never even got a chance to start.

My eyes burn with unshed tears. I blink them back, refusing to cry in the backseat of an Uber. I've never cried over a man before, and I'm not about to start now. This is exactly why I've avoided relationships all these years—the mess, the pain, the distraction.

I need to focus on the showcase. On my auditions. On my future career. David Hunter was just a detour, a temporary pleasure that turned into something I never signed up for.

So why can't I stop thinking about him? About the way his eyes crinkled when he laughed, or how he always seemed to know exactly where to touch me, or the gentle way he'd stroke my hair when he thought I was sleeping?

The car stops outside my dorm, and I mumble a thank you to the driver before climbing out. The building looks the same as always, but I feel changed, like I'm returning a different person than the one who left.

I check my phone one last time before going inside.

Still nothing.

Maybe this is what growing up feels like—realizing that some emotions are too big, too scary to face. That sometimes the smartest choice is to run away before you get in too deep.

Or maybe I'm just a coward.

I take a deep breath and push through the building's main door. Whatever I'm feeling, I'll bury it. I'll focus on my lines, my auditions, my dreams. I've come too far to let a man—even one who makes me feel things I've never felt before—derail my plans.

I'll forget David Hunter. I have to.

But as the elevator climbs to my floor, I can't help wondering if that's even possible. Because the truth—the terrifying, undeniable truth—is that I'm already in love with him.

And I'm pretty sure I just walked away from the best thing that ever happened to me.

FOURTEEN

Best Part of Me

WHITNEY BARNES

THE SPOTLIGHT'S heat falls like liquid fire across my skin as I deliver my final line, the words hanging in momentary silence before Quinn steps forward with her response. We're halfway through the third act of "Tomorrow's Horizon," and despite the sweat threatening to ruin my stage makeup and the slight pinch of these vintage shoes, I've never felt more alive.

"You can't possibly understand what it means to leave everything behind," I proclaim, my voice carrying to the back row of the packed auditorium.

Quinn steps toward me, her green eyes flashing with practiced indignation beneath the stage lights. Her blonde hair is styled in a perfect 1940s wave, and her period costume fits her like it was made for her body alone.

"Then make me understand," she replies, her voice breaking just enough to indicate her character's desperation.

I turn away, giving the audience my profile as I learned in Professor Lambert's direction class. "Some journeys can only be walked alone, Caroline."

The exchange continues as we weave through our scene, the other actors moving around us in choreographed precision. My body feels electric, every nerve ending alive with the thrill of performance. This is what I was born to do. This feeling—this rush—it's better than sex, better than...

David's face flashes unbidden in my mind, and I falter for just a millisecond before recovering. No. Not now. I push him from my thoughts, focusing instead on the culmination of weeks of exhausting rehearsals.

For the next twenty minutes, I am not Whitney Barnes pretending to be someone else. I am Eliza Carmichael, a woman torn between family obligations and pursuing her dreams in a time when women were expected to know their place. The parallels to my own life aren't lost on me, but I channel that tension into my performance.

When the final scene arrives, I stand center stage, suitcase in hand, ready to board a train to my character's uncertain future. The lights dim slowly as the narrator delivers the epilogue, and in that darkness, I feel a single tear escape down my cheek—not scripted, not planned, just real.

Then silence. Complete, terrifying silence, before—

Thunder. The applause hits like a physical force, startling in its intensity. The lights come up for curtain call, and my cast mates join hands as we step forward to take our bows. Quinn squeezes my fingers tight as we dip in unison, and I catch glimpses of people rising to their feet in the audience.

A standing ovation.

Professor Lambert, our director, joins us onstage, his normally stern face cracked wide with a smile I've rarely seen. He gestures to all of us with obvious pride as the applause continues.

"Ladies and gentlemen, the talented cast of 'Tomorrow's Horizon'!" he announces into the microphone someone has handed him. "These extraordinary young actors have worked tirelessly to bring this production to life. Please, another round of applause!"

The audience obliges enthusiastically. I scan the faces reflexively, looking for—no, I'm not looking for him. I'm not.

After final bows, we rush backstage in a chaotic flood of adrenaline and elation. Bodies press against each other in tight hugs, exclamations and congratulations flowing freely. Quinn wraps her arms around me, jumping up and down like we're five years old.

"We fucking did it!" she squeals. "You were amazing, Whit! That moment in the third act where you—"

"Ladies." Professor Lambert appears beside us, accompanied by a man and woman I don't recognize. Both are dressed impeccably in what I immediately identify as New York fashion—understated but expensive. "If I might interrupt your celebration briefly. Whitney Barnes, Quinn Hunter, I'd like you to meet Elaine Wittman and Marcus Devereaux from The Broadway Workshop."

My heart stutters. The Broadway Workshop—only the most prestigious young actors' program in New York. A direct pipeline to auditions that normal drama students would never get.

Elaine extends her hand first, her grip firm and professional. "Ms. Barnes, your performance tonight was extraordinary. The emotional honesty in your portrayal was quite remarkable for someone your age."

"Thank you," I manage, my throat suddenly dry.

Marcus nods in agreement. "We don't often venture this far from New York for college productions, but Professor Lambert has been singing your praises for months. I'm pleased to say he wasn't exaggerating."

Quinn nudges me slightly, a silent cue to say something intelligent.

"I'm honored you came all this way," I reply, trying to sound professional despite the stage makeup still caked on my face and the sweat cooling beneath my costume.

Elaine smiles. "We don't make the trip unless we believe it's worth our time. Ms. Barnes, we'd like to offer you a position in our summer intensive program. All expenses paid. Six weeks in New York working with Broadway directors, casting agents, and performers."

The world tilts slightly. All expenses paid. New York. Broadway connections.

"This is a highly selective opportunity," Marcus adds. "Only twelve actors are chosen nationwide each year."

Professor Lambert beams beside them. "This is an incredible opportunity, Whitney."

Quinn's hand finds mine, squeezing so hard it hurts. I barely notice.

"When would I need to let you know?" I ask, trying to sound like someone who needs to consider multiple offers rather than someone whose brain is screaming YES YES YES.

"We'll need confirmation within the week," Elaine says, reaching into her elegant leather portfolio to extract a card. "All the details are in the packet we'll email tomorrow, but feel free to call with questions."

I take the card, trying to keep my fingers from trembling. "Thank you. I'll review everything carefully."

After exchanging a few more pleasantries, they move on to speak with Professor Lambert about the production values of the show. The moment they're out of earshot, Quinn grabs both my shoulders.

"Holy fuck, Whitney!" she whisper-screams. "The Broadway Workshop? All expenses paid? Do you have any idea—"

"I know," I whisper back, my voice unsteady. "I know exactly what this means."

It means everything. It means a foot in the door that most people spend years trying to squeeze through. It means connections, training, and exposure to people who can change my life with a single phone call.

It means leaving for the summer. Leaving Quinn. Leaving...

The celebration continues around us as we change out of our costumes and remove our stage makeup. Friends and family filter backstage with flowers and congratulations. Quinn's mother appears with a bouquet for each of us, gushing over our performances. I scan the crowd behind her automatically, feeling a sharp pang when I don't see him.

Later, after most people have left for the cast party at Randall's apartment off-campus, Quinn and I linger in the now-quiet dressing room.

"So," she says, applying lip gloss in the mirror, "you're going to New York."

It's not a question. She knows me too well.

"I haven't even seen the official offer yet," I hedge.

Quinn turns, fixing me with a look. "Cut the crap, Whitney. This is literally everything you've ever wanted. Of course, you're going."

I sink onto the worn couch in the corner. "Yeah. I'm going."

She sits beside me, taking my hand. "I'm so, so happy for you. This is huge, Whit. This is meant to be."

"Really? You're not upset about me leaving for the summer?"

Quinn laughs. "Are you kidding? I'm going to visit you in New York and make you take me to all the cool places regular tourists never see." She bumps my shoulder with hers. "I expect backstage Broadway tickets when you're famous, by the way."

I lean my head against her shoulder, suddenly emotional. "Thank you for being happy for me."

"Always," she replies, then hesitates. "Have you thought about... what this means for you and David?"

The name hits me like a physical blow. "There is no 'me and David.'"

"Whitney—"

"We haven't spoken in almost three weeks," I interrupt, pulling away slightly. "Not since that night."

The memory of waking up in his arms, feeling terrified

by how right it felt, how I fled his apartment like I was running from a fire—it all comes rushing back.

"Has he..." I swallow hard, hating my own vulnerability. "Is David okay?"

Quinn studies me for a long moment. "You haven't heard from him?"

I shake my head, looking down at my hands. "No. Nothing."

"I could talk to him," she offers carefully. "See where his head's at."

"No." The word comes out sharper than I intended. "No, don't. Please." I take a deep breath. "It's better this way. We agreed from the beginning—no complications. This is for the best."

Even as I say it, I feel hollow. But I've worked too hard, come too far to let anything—or anyone—derail me now. New York is calling. My dreams are calling.

"If you're sure," Quinn says, squeezing my hand once more.

"I'm sure," I lie, and try to ignore the ache in my chest that feels suspiciously like missing someone I never planned to miss at all.

* * *

I HIT SEND ON the email with surprisingly steady fingers, though my heart's hammering against my ribs like it's trying to escape. The Broadway Workshop application is officially accepted, my confirmation sent, my fate sealed. I'm going to New York. I'm actually going to New York.

For a moment I just sit there on my bed, laptop balanced on my knees, waiting for the rush of pure joy I've always imagined would accompany this moment. Instead, I feel something more complicated—excitement tangled with anxiety, triumph laced with an unexpected melancholy.

"Get it together, Whitney," I mutter to myself, closing the laptop and setting it aside.

My suitcases are already laid out on the floor, one large and one small. Summer in New York means packing smart—versatile pieces that can transition from daytime workshops to evening networking events. I've been planning this wardrobe in my head for years, even when it was just a fantasy.

I fold a sleek black dress that can be dressed up or down and place it carefully in the larger suitcase. The fabric feels expensive against my fingers, a splurge from last semester when I landed that local commercial gig. Six weeks in New York. The thought alone sends electricity through my veins.

My phone buzzes with a text from Quinn.

> Quinn: Staying at Tyler's tonight. Don't wait up! SO PROUD OF YOU!!!

I text back a quick thanks and a heart emoji, then glance around our empty dorm room. Quinn's side is its usual organized chaos—clothes draped over her desk chair, textbooks stacked haphazardly, fairy lights strung above her bed that she insists help her sleep. My side is neater, more minimalist, though currently disrupted by the packing process.

The silence feels heavier than usual tonight. No Quinn chattering about her day or playing her endless playlists of early 2000s pop music that she claims are "vintage" now. Just me and the distant sounds of other students moving through the hallway outside.

I reach for my phone again, scrolling through my notifications like I'm looking for something specific. I'm not. I'm definitely not.

But my thumb hovers betrayingly over his name in my contacts. David. Not Jax anymore—that fantasy was shattered the moment I saw him sprawled across his family's couch at Thanksgiving. David Hunter. Quinn's brother. The man I've been deliberately not thinking about for twenty days straight. Not that I'm counting.

"This is pathetic," I tell the empty room, tossing my phone onto the bed like it's suddenly burned me.

I turn back to my suitcase with renewed determination, pulling items from my closet with efficient movements. Summer tops, lightweight pants, that one floral skirt that always gets me compliments. I fold each piece with precision, arranging them in neat rows.

But as I work, my mind wanders. Not to New York or Broadway or the career I've been chasing since I was eight years old. No, it drifts to moments I've been trying to forget—David's laugh when I told him about my disastrous first audition freshman year. The way his fingers traced patterns on my bare back in the darkness of his apartment. The focused intensity in his eyes when he actually listened to me talk about my dreams, never once dismissing them as impossible the way my mother always does.

I shake my head sharply, as if I can physically dislodge these memories. "Focus, Whitney."

My jewelry case is next—I carefully select pieces that can elevate simple outfits. The delicate gold necklace my grandmother gave me before she died. The statement earrings I found at a vintage shop downtown.

My phone buzzes again from the bed. For one heart-stopping moment, I think—hope?—it might be him. But it's just an email notification from The Broadway Workshop with pre-arrival information.

I sink onto the edge of my bed, suddenly exhausted. The room feels too quiet, too empty. I reach for my phone again, scrolling mindlessly through social media without really seeing anything. My thumb hovers over the Instagram search bar, and before I can stop myself, I type his name.

David's profile appears immediately. He's not particularly active on social media, which used to frustrate me when I was trying to figure out who he really was beyond "Jax." His last post is from three weeks ago—a picture of him with his engineering classmates after some project presentation. He's smiling, but it doesn't reach his eyes the way it does when he's genuinely happy. I know that face too well.

I close Instagram quickly, feeling like I've crossed some invisible boundary. This is exactly what I wasn't going to do. This sentimentality, this looking backward instead of forward—it's not who I am. It's not who I've ever been.

And yet.

The emptiness of the room presses in on me. Quinn's absence feels particularly acute tonight, like the universe deliberately removing my buffer against myself. Without her chatter and energy filling the space, I'm left alone with thoughts I've been outrunning for weeks.

I pick up my phone again, this time opening my text messages. My conversation with David sits there, unchanged since that morning I left his apartment. The last text is from him, sent about an hour after I'd rushed out:

> David: Come back

I never responded. *What was there to say? That I panicked? That waking up in his arms felt too real, too right? That I could suddenly picture a future stretching out before us that terrified me precisely because I wanted it?*

My thumbs hover over the keyboard now. It would be so easy to text him. To say... what? *Hey, I'm moving to New York for the summer. Just thought you should know.* Or maybe, *I miss you and I don't know why.* Or the most dangerous truth of all: *I think I'm in love with you and it scares the hell out of me.*

I close my eyes, letting my head fall back against the wall behind me. This is exactly what I've been avoiding. This weakness. This distraction. I've worked too hard, sacrificed too much to let myself get derailed now. My entire life has been aimed toward this moment, this opportunity. The Broadway Workshop is everything I've ever wanted.

Isn't it?

The question sends a jolt through me, unwelcome and unsettling. Of course it is. This is my dream. This is what I've been fighting for against my mother's disapproval, against the statistics stacked against every aspiring actress, against my own doubts in the darkest hours of the night.

So why am I sitting here staring at a text conversation that ended three weeks ago, feeling like I'm leaving something essential behind?

"You're being ridiculous," I say aloud, my voice harsh in the quiet room. "This was never supposed to be anything serious."

But it became serious, didn't it? Somewhere between the fake names and the late-night conversations and the way David looked at me when he thought I wouldn't notice. Somewhere between the laughter and the arguments and how he never once made me feel like my dreams were too big or too unrealistic. It became real when I wasn't looking.

I place my phone face down on the nightstand, a deliberate action. Then I stand and return to my packing, movements more mechanical now. The Broadway Workshop is waiting. New York is waiting. Everything I've ever worked for is finally within reach.

So why does it suddenly feel like I'm running away rather than running toward something?

Because I am in love with David Hunter, the realization doesn't crash over me like a wave; it simply rises to the surface like it's been there all along, waiting to be acknowledged. I love his quick wit and the way his mind works. I love how he sees me—really sees me—not just as a body, not just as Quinn's roommate, but as a woman with dreams and fears and talent.

I love him, and I'm leaving anyway.

Because that's the choice, isn't it? Love or ambition.

David or New York. The unexpected complication or the dream I've chased my entire life.

I close the suitcase with a decisive zip, swallowing the lump in my throat. Some choices make themselves. Some dreams demand everything. And I've never been the kind of woman who chooses a man over her future.

Even if that choice feels, for the first time in my life, like I might be leaving the best part of me behind.

FIFTEEN

Like a Physical Blow

DAVID HUNTER

THE TEXTBOOK BLURS in front of me. Fluid mechanics should be fascinating—it's literally about how things flow and change shape under pressure. Just like my life right now. But I can't focus worth a damn.

I slam the book closed, earning glares from the students around me in the engineering library. Whatever. Let them judge. Two all-nighters this week and I'm still behind on assignments.

My phone buzzes. Another text from Jake about tonight's party at Sigma Chi.

> Jake: Dude. Three kegs. Sorority mixer. You're coming.

I stare at it for a few seconds before typing back:

> David: Maybe. Buried in work.

That's been my response to everything lately. Maybe. Which means no, but I don't want to explain why. Because explaining why means admitting things I'm not ready to face.

It's been twenty-three days since I last saw Whitney. Not that I'm counting.

Twenty-three days since she bolted from my apartment like I was contagious. Twenty-three days of checking my phone like some lovesick teenager, hoping to see her name pop up.

Hell, I even drove by the theater department last week, telling myself I was just passing through campus. Pathetic.

I pack up my stuff, giving up on studying. Outside, the December air hits my face, sharp and cold. Christmas break is coming up. Another two weeks of pretending I'm fine at my parents' house while my dad works and my mom tries to figure out why I'm not my usual charming self.

My phone buzzes again. Quinn.

> Quinn: You alive?

I type back:

> David: Unfortunately

The phone rings immediately. I consider not answering, but it's Quinn.

"What crawled up your ass and died?" she asks without preamble.

"Good to hear your voice too, sis."

"Seriously, David. You sound like crap, you look like crap—"

"You can't see me."

"I saw you last weekend when you came home. Mom's worried."

I kick at a pile of dead leaves. "I'm fine. Just busy with finals."

"Bullshit. This is about Whitney."

The sound of her name makes my chest tighten. "How is she?" The question slips out before I can stop it.

"Why don't you ask her yourself?"

"I've been busy."

"Too busy to text? Please."

I stop walking, leaning against a lamppost. "She's the one who left, Quinn. Not me."

"And you're the one who's too chicken to reach out. You're both idiots."

"Did she say something about me?" I hate how eager I sound.

Quinn sighs dramatically. "I told you last week. *'You need to talk to her.'* That's all I'm saying. I'm not your relationship counselor."

"We don't have a relationship."

"Keep telling yourself that."

After Quinn hangs up, I stand there like an idiot, staring at my phone. Pull it together, Hunter. This is exactly what you swore you'd never do again. Not after Madison.

Madison with her pretty lies and the way she made me believe we had something real, only to find her screwing my best friend. That broke something in me. Made me promise myself I'd never give anyone that power again.

But Whitney... Whitney is different.

I start walking again, faster this time, like I can outrun my thoughts.

Back at my apartment, my roommate Ryder is on the couch playing Call of Duty. He barely glances up as I walk in.

"You look like shit."

"Thanks."

"There's pizza in the fridge if you want it."

I grab a cold slice and sink into the chair, watching him blow up digital enemies.

"Jake texted. Party tonight," Ryder says, eyes still on the screen.

"I know."

"We're going."

"I don't—"

"Dude." Ryder pauses the game and turns to me. "You haven't gone out in weeks. You barely talk. You just study and brood. It's depressing as hell."

"I don't brood."

"You're brooding right now. Look, whatever's going on with you and that girl—"

"There's no girl."

"—you need to either fix it or move on. Starting tonight."

I take a bite of pizza to avoid responding. Ryder's right, and we both know it. This isn't me. I'm David Hunter. I don't pine over women. I'm the guy who keeps it casual. The guy who has fun without complications.

Except nothing feels fun anymore.

"Fine," I finally say. "One beer. Then I'm coming back to study."

Ryder grins. "That's what you said last time, and we ended up at Waffle House at 4 AM."

"That was before finals."

"Whatever. Just be ready by ten."

I drag myself to the shower, hoping hot water will wash away this funk. As the spray hits my face, my mind drifts back to Whitney. The way she looked in the morning light, all sleep-soft and beautiful. The way she laughed at my dumb jokes. The way she was real with me, not just the hookup girl "Nikki" but Whitney—smart, ambitious, complicated.

The way she ran out like I was poison.

Does she need to speak to me? I replay our last time together. We'd had amazing sex—different somehow. More intense. More... everything. Then she looked at me like she'd seen a ghost and couldn't get away fast enough.

What was I supposed to do with that?

Pride kept me from texting her. That and fear. Fear that whatever I saw in her eyes that morning was real—that she'd realized this thing between us had grown beyond what either of us signed up for, and she wanted no part of it.

I turn off the water and wrap a towel around my waist. My phone sits on the counter, tempting me. Just text her. Something casual. *Hey, how's it going? How'd the play turn out?*

The play...

I sit in the theater, wedged between my mother and some guy wearing too much cologne, and try to look casual. Like I just happen to be here supporting my sister Quinn, not secretly hoping to catch a glimpse of the woman who's hijacked my thoughts for weeks.

"Isn't this exciting?" Mom whispers, squeezing my arm.

I nod, pretending to read the program for the third time. Quinn's name is right there: Quinn Hunter as "Eliza." And below it, the name I've been avoiding saying out loud: Whitney Barnes as "Catherine."

The lights dim. I feel my pulse quicken. Get it together, Hunter.

The curtain rises, revealing a minimalist set—a few chairs, a table, some abstract backdrop representing a living room. Quinn enters first, and Mom clutches my arm tighter. My sister looks different up there, more confident somehow. I hear Mom whisper, "That's my girl," and I feel a flash of pride.

Then Whitney walks onstage, and everything else fades.

She's transformed, not just by the period costume she's wearing, but by her entire presence. Her voice fills the theater, clear and commanding. Her movements are precise, deliberate. This isn't the Whitney who laughed in my bed or argued with me in my kitchen—this is someone else entirely, someone fully inhabiting another person's skin.

I lean forward without realizing it. She's magnetic. When she delivers an emotional monologue about betrayal in the second act, I feel it like a physical blow. The raw vulnerability on her face makes my chest ache.

Is she thinking about us?

Stop it. This isn't about you. She's acting. That's the whole point.

But watching her up there, something shifts inside me. I always knew Whitney was talented—she'd talked about it enough—but seeing is different. She's not just good. She's extraordinary. She belongs up there, shining under those lights, commanding the audience's attention.

During intermission, Mom turns to me. "Quinn's roommate is incredibly talented, don't you think?"

"Yeah," I manage. "She's really good."

Mom studies my face with that look mothers get when they're connecting dots you wish they wouldn't connect. "She seems like a lovely girl."

"I wouldn't know."

The second act is even more intense than the first. Whitney's character confronts her lover about his betrayal. The rage and hurt in her voice cut through me. When she cries, real tears stream down her face. I know it's acting, but holy shit, it feels real.

I wonder if Quinn told her I'd be here tonight. If Whitney's performing knowing I'm watching. If some part of this performance is meant for me.

But that's narcissistic bullshit, isn't it? Whitney's career ambitions were clear from day one. This performance isn't about me or us—it's about her future. About proving she has what it takes to make it.

And she does. No question.

When the play ends, the audience erupts in applause. We all stand, and I clap until my hands hurt. Mom is beaming with pride, not just for Quinn but seemingly for all the performers. When Whitney takes her bow, there's an extra surge of applause. She's made an impression, not just on me.

"We should go backstage to congratulate them," Mom says as people begin filing out.

My stomach drops. "You go ahead. I'll meet you at the car."

Her expression shifts to disappointment. "David, don't be ridiculous. Quinn will want to see you."

"I don't want to get in the way of her moment."

"She's your sister."

I can't explain to my mother that I'm afraid of seeing Whitney up close. Afraid of what might show on my face, or worse, what might not show on hers.

But Mom's already pulling me along, navigating through the crowd toward the backstage area. People are clutching bouquets, congratulating each other. The energy is electric—vibrant with success and relief.

Quinn spots us first. She's still in costume, face flushed with post-performance adrenaline.

"You came!" She throws her arms around me, then Mom. "Did you love it? Was I amazing? Be honest."

"You were wonderful, darling," Mom gushes, pulling out a small bouquet of roses she'd been hiding in her purse.

"You didn't suck," I tease, earning a punch in the arm. Same old Quinn, even in costume.

I scan the room over Quinn's shoulder, trying to be subtle. There are actors everywhere, hugging friends, taking photos. But no Whitney.

"She went to change," Quinn says quietly, catching my wandering gaze. There's something knowing in her eyes. "The producers from The Broadway Workshop wanted to talk to her after the show."

"What's that?"

"Only the most prestigious young actors' program in New York." Quinn's voice carries a mixture of pride and envy. "They're offering her a full scholarship. All expenses paid."

My heart sinks and soars simultaneously. New York. That's what, a thousand miles away? But it's what she always wanted. What she deserves.

"That's... incredible," I manage.

"She's leaving for the summer," Quinn adds. Her eyes are searching my face, looking for a reaction.

I keep my expression neutral through sheer force of will. "Good for her."

Mom, oblivious to the undercurrents, is chatting with one of Quinn's castmates. Quinn lowers her voice. "You know, you could still talk to her before she leaves."

"What makes you think I want to?"

"Oh please, David. You've been moping for weeks. It's embarrassing."

"I don't mope."

"Then what do you call ignoring parties, skipping family dinners, and looking like someone ran over your puppy?"

I scoff. "Finals are kicking my ass. Not everyone majors in pretending to be other people."

The barb lands. Quinn's expression hardens. "At least I don't pretend with myself."

Before I can respond, someone calls Quinn's name. She gives me one last meaningful look before rejoining her theater friends, leaving me alone with my thoughts.

I drift toward the exit, needing air. The lobby is emptying out, just a few stragglers checking their phones or waiting for performers.

My mind races with possibilities. I could wait for Whitney to emerge. Say something casual, congratulate her on her performance and the New York opportunity. Be the bigger person.

But what would be the point? She made her choice that morning in my apartment. The look in her eyes before she fled told me everything I needed to know. Whatever was building between us scared her. And maybe she was right to be scared. We both said no complications.

New York would be her fresh start. Her big break. Who am I to stand in the way of that?

I head outside, texting Mom that I'll wait in the car. The summer air is warm, heating my cheeks. I look up at the theater building, imagining Whitney inside, still riding the high of her performance, maybe already dreaming of Broadway lights.

Pride swells in my chest, surprising me with its intensity. She was magnificent up there. I've never seen anyone so completely in their element, so clearly born to do something. Whitney on stage isn't just talented—she's transcendent.

And isn't that the cruel irony? I finally find someone who gets under my skin, who makes me question everything I thought I knew about what I wanted, and she's about to fly away, chasing a dream that has nothing to do with me.

I lean against my car, watching people exit the theater in twos and threes, laughing and chatting about the performance. No sign of Whitney. Maybe she's still talking to those producers. Maybe she left through another exit.

Maybe it's better this way. No awkward confrontation. No forced small talk that doesn't begin to address what happened between us.

Instead, I'll remember her like this: brilliant and alive, commanding the stage, showing everyone exactly why she deserves every opportunity coming her way. I'll remember the pride I felt watching her shine, even as something inside me cracked at the realization that the things that make her special are the very things that will take her away from here. Away from any possibility of us.

I GET DRESSED MECHANICALLY, mind still circling the same questions. By the time Ryder bangs on my door yelling that the Uber's five minutes away, I've changed shirts three times and still look like I couldn't care less.

The party is exactly what you'd expect from Sigma Chi in May. String lights strung haphazardly. Pitchers of something red and potent. Music too loud. Bodies too close.

I grab a beer and find myself a corner, nodding to people I know but not engaging. Ryder gives me concerned looks between chatting up a redhead from his economics class.

An hour in, I'm on my third beer when someone taps my shoulder.

"You look thrilled to be here."

I turn to find Alicia, a girl from my thermodynamics class. She's pretty, with dark curls and a dangerous smile.

"Just taking in the atmosphere," I say, gesturing to the chaos around us.

"You've been taking it in from this exact spot for forty-five minutes." She moves closer. "Not your usual style, Hunter."

Not my usual style. That about sums up everything lately.

"Maybe I'm evolving," I say with a half-smile.

"Into what? A statue?" She touches my arm lightly. "Dance with me. One song. Then you can go back to your brooding corner."

I don't brood.

But I let her pull me toward the dancing mass of bodies anyway. The song is something with a heavy bass that you feel more than hear. Alicia moves against me, her hands finding my shoulders.

A month ago, I'd have been all in. Flirting back. Enjoying the attention. Now I'm just going through the motions.

"You're somewhere else tonight," she says in my ear, not accusatory, just observant.

"Sorry."

"Don't be. Whoever she is, she did a number on you."

I step back slightly. "What makes you think there's a she?"

Alicia laughs. "Please. You've turned down Brianna Matthews twice this semester. Only love or brain damage explains that."

"Maybe it's brain damage."

"Nah. You're still acing exams. It's definitely love."

The word hits me like a physical blow. *Love.* Is that what this is? This constant ache. This inability to focus. This feeling that nothing's quite right in my world?

Shit. I'm in love with Whitney.

The realization doesn't surprise me as much as it should. Maybe I've known for weeks, just been too stubborn to admit it.

"I need some air," I tell Alicia, already backing away.

Outside, the cold feels good after the stuffy heat of the party. I lean against the fraternity house porch railing and pull out my phone. It's almost midnight.

Before I can overthink it, I pull up Whitney's contact. My thumb hovers over her name. *What would I even say?*

I miss you. I think about you constantly. I'm scared of what I feel for you.

I lock the screen and shove the phone back in my pocket. This is why I don't do relationships. They make you vulnerable. Weak. And when they end—because they always end—you're left with pieces of yourself missing.

Just like with Madison.

But Whitney isn't Madison. I know that. Madison was calculated. Whitney is real. Too real, sometimes. Maybe that's what scares her too.

Ryder finds me outside twenty minutes later.

"Dude, you okay?"

"Yeah." I straighten up. "Just needed a break."

"From Alicia? She's hot."

"She's nice."

Ryder gives me a long look. "You're really messed up over this girl, aren't you?"

"What girl?" I try, but my voice lacks conviction.

"Quinn's roommate. The one you hook up with. The one you've been sulking over for weeks."

"I don't sulk."

"You're literally sulking right now on a porch while hot, willing women are inside."

He's not wrong. What's happened to me?

"I think I'm done for tonight," I tell him. "Going to head home."

"Alone?"

"Yes, alone. I've got an 8 AM final."

Ryder shakes his head but doesn't argue. "Your call. But David?"

"Yeah?"

"Either call her or move on. This in-between shit is depressing to watch."

He goes back inside, leaving me with his words echoing in my head. Call her or move on. Those are my options.

Problem is, I don't think I can do either one.

SIXTEEN

Run From Love
WHITNEY BARNES

Six months later

THE JUNE HEAT in New York is different from back home—it's like the buildings trap it, intensifying everything until the air between skyscrapers shimmers. I stand at the window of my tiny sublet in Hell's Kitchen, forehead pressed against the glass despite the warmth radiating through it. Six floors below, the street pulses with that unmistakable Manhattan energy I've grown to love.

Six months. Half a year since I packed two suitcases and kissed Quinn goodbye at the airport. Half a year of subway rides, voice lessons, movement classes, and a hunger so deep in my bones it sometimes keeps me awake at night.

My phone buzzes with a text from Jamal, my castmate.

> Jamal: You ready for this? Last rehearsal before previews!

I type back with thumbs that suddenly feel clumsy:

> Whitney: Born ready. See you there.

The truth is more complicated. Am I ready to be on a real Off-Broadway stage? Yes and no and yes again. The Broadway Workshop changed everything. What started as a three-month intensive program turned into the opportunity I'd been dreaming about since I was seven years old with a hairbrush microphone. When Director Marcus Holt approached me after our final showcase and offered me the role of Delilah in his new production, I nearly fainted right there on the spot.

"It's a supporting role," he'd said, hands gesturing expressively, "but it's pivotal. The audience needs to fall in love with Delilah before the betrayal in Act Two lands with full impact."

I remember nodding, trying to look professional while screaming internally.

I gulp down the last of my lukewarm coffee, grimacing at the bitter dregs. My reflection in the bathroom mirror looks back at me—hair grown out a bit from my usual short cut, dark circles under my eyes, but there's something else there too. A certainty that wasn't there before.

My phone rings. It's Mama.

"Whitney Barnes, is your parent still on the guest list for opening night?" She asks without preamble, her voice crackling through the speaker.

"Yes, Mama. Front row center, just like I promised." I cradle the phone between my ear and shoulder while rummaging through my closet for a clean tank top.

"And Whitney, baby," there's a pause, and I can picture her straightening her shoulders the way she does when she's about to say something meaningful. "I am proud of you."

The words catch me off guard. My mother—the pragmatic business executive who spent years trying to steer me toward accounting—has done a complete one-eighty since the workshop. Now she's my biggest cheerleader, sending care packages with throat lozenges and clipped reviews of shows similar to mine.

"Thanks, Mama." I swallow around the sudden lump in my throat. "That means a lot."

"Have you heard from Quinn lately?" she asks, changing subjects with her typical efficiency.

My stomach does that familiar flip at the mere adjacency to thoughts of David. "We talked yesterday. She's coming for closing night with her mom."

What I don't say: I asked, in what I hoped was a casual way, whether David would be joining them. Quinn just said, "He's busy with his engineering internship," and quickly changed the subject.

I've gotten good at pretending that's fine.

"Well, break a leg at rehearsal. Call me tonight?"

After hanging up, I stuff script pages into my backpack alongside a water bottle and granola bars. The subway is crowded despite the midday hour, bodies pressed together in shared discomfort. I close my eyes and run lines in my head, mouthing them silently as the train rumbles beneath the city.

The theater smells like dust and possibility when I push through the stage door. It's small by Broadway standards —only 220 seats—but to me, it's everything. My footsteps echo as I cross the stage, running my fingers along the partially constructed set pieces.

"There she is! Our Delilah in the flesh!" Marcus's voice booms from the house, where he sits with his laptop perched on his knees. "How are we feeling about tomorrow, Whitney?"

"Like I might throw up, but in a good way," I answer honestly, dropping my bag in the wings.

He laughs, the sound bouncing off the walls. "That's the appropriate response. Channel it."

The rest of the cast filters in—Jamal and Tessa, who play the leads; Riccardo, our villain; and the ensemble members who've become my New York family. We warm up together, bodies stretching and voices rising in scales that intertwine and separate.

During the run-through, I lose myself completely. Delilah—the charming best friend with a secret agenda—takes over, and for two glorious hours, I'm not Whitney Barnes from back home. I'm not the girl who fell for her roommate's brother and then ran away to New York. I'm just Delilah, navigating the complexities of her world with nuance and intention.

When I deliver my pivotal monologue in Act Two—the one where Delilah reveals why she betrayed her best friend—I feel something click into place that's been just slightly off until now. The words flow through me as if I've lived them, each sentence carrying the weight of my own unspoken regrets.

"Sometimes," I say to Tessa's character, my voice barely above a whisper, "we run from love not because we don't feel it, but because we feel it too much."

When I finish, the theater is eerily silent. Then Marcus stands, clapping slowly.

"That," he says, "is exactly what we've been looking for."

Later, as we gather our things, Tessa bumps my shoulder with hers. "You okay? That monologue was intense today."

I nod, zipping up my bag. "Just found the connection, I guess."

"Well, whatever you tapped into, keep it close. It was magic."

Outside, the day has cooled slightly, the early evening bringing a gentle breeze through the concrete corridors. I decide to walk part of the way home, needing to feel the city against my skin.

My phone buzzes with a notification from social media—Quinn has tagged me in a post. It's a throwback photo from last fall, before everything changed. We're in costume for the university production, arms around each other, laughing at something off-camera. The caption reads: *Counting down the days until I see this superstar on stage! #ProudBestFriend #OffBroadwayBound*

I zoom in on the photo, noticing details I'd forgotten. The way my eyes crinkled at the corners. The vibrant energy captured in that single moment.

I keep walking, pocketing my phone. New York stretches around me—all possibility and promise and dreams fulfilled. This is everything I wanted. The path I chose.

So why does it sometimes feel like I'm still running?

My sublet building comes into view, and I check my mailbox out of habit, not expecting anything. There's a thick cream-colored envelope with my name written in elegant cursive. The return address says "The Whitfield Foundation for the Arts."

I tear it open right there in the lobby, heart hammering. The Whitfield Foundation is one of the most prestigious arts organizations in the country, known for identifying and supporting emerging talent.

Dear Ms. Barnes,

We are pleased to inform you that you have been selected as one of five recipients of this year's Breakthrough Performer Grant. This award includes a financial stipend of $25,000 and mentorship opportunities with established Broadway performers...

The words blur as tears fill my eyes. This changes everything—the grant means I can stay in New York after the show closes, take the masterclasses I couldn't afford, audition without the constant panic about making rent.

THE SPOTLIGHT FADES, and the warmth of it lingers on my skin as I make my way backstage. My heart still drums against my ribs, riding the high of another performance. Six months in New York. Six months living my dream.

The narrow corridors of the theater buzz with post-show energy—stagehands rushing past, cast members exchanging congratulations. I nod and smile, accepting their praise with a practiced grace that still feels foreign on my shoulders.

"Killed it tonight, Whitney!" Marcus, one of the supporting actors, high-fives me as he passes.

"Thanks," I say, the single word barely capturing the electric rush coursing through me.

My dressing room—small but mine—waits at the end of the hallway. The little star-shaped nameplate reads "Whitney Barnes" in gold letters. Every time I see it, I feel like I'm floating. I trace my finger over the letters before pushing the door open.

Inside, the mirror surrounded by bare bulbs casts a harsh glow over everything. Flowers from tonight's performance crowd my makeup table—roses from the director, a mixed arrangement from the cast. The smell of them mixes with grease paint and setting spray.

I sink into my chair, kicking off my heels with a groan. My feet ache in the best possible way. War wounds from chasing my dream. Who knew standing on stage for two hours could hurt so good?

I reach for my phone, scrolling through notifications. Three texts from Quinn, congratulating me on tonight's show. She's been my rock through all of this, video-calling me at least twice a week, listening to all my stories about New York and Broadway and everything in between. She never mentions him, though. That's our unspoken rule.

My fingers pause over the screen, and I set the phone down. Even thinking his name makes something twist inside me, like someone's wringing out my heart. Six months should be enough time to forget someone, right? Especially someone I never actually dated.

"Never actually dated," I mutter to myself, reaching up to unpin my wig. "Just had the best sex of your life with and maybe fell completely in love with."

The pins come out one by one, and I carefully lift the wig from my head, revealing my own hair pressed flat underneath. I stare at my reflection—at the girl who left everything behind for this dream. College. Friends. Maybe love.

Was it worth it?

The question haunts me on nights like these when the applause fades and I'm left alone with myself. I think about the life I might have had if I'd stayed. If I'd chosen David instead of Broadway.

"Of course it was worth it," I tell my reflection firmly. "Look at you."

And it's true. I'm doing what I've always wanted. I'm making a name for myself. The reviews for our show have been stellar, and my small role has earned more than one positive mention. I've got a tiny apartment in Hell's Kitchen that costs more than some people's mortgages, but it's mine. I've got freedom. I've got potential.

So why does it still sting when I think about what could have been?

I reach for my makeup wipes, dragging one across my forehead to remove the stage foundation. My movements are practiced, almost mechanical. Forehead, cheeks, chin, nose. Wipe away the character and find Whitney underneath.

"You made the right choice," I murmur, watching my features emerge from beneath the heavy makeup. "No complications, remember? Just like you wanted."

But what if what I wanted then isn't what I want now?

I close my eyes, and for a moment, I let myself remember. David's hands on my skin. The way he looked at me that afternoon in his apartment, like I was the answer to a question he'd been asking his whole life. The heat between us—not just physical, though God knows that was enough to burn down a city block—but something deeper. Something that scared the hell out of me.

When I open my eyes again, I see him in the mirror.

David.

Standing in my doorway, one shoulder leaned against the frame like he belongs there. Like no time has passed at all.

My heart stops, then races. I blink hard, certain I'm hallucinating. Too many late nights, too much wishful thinking. But when I look again, he's still there.

I whip around so fast my neck cracks, and there's no mistaking it—David Hunter is *really* here, in my dressing room, looking at me with those hazel eyes that have haunted my dreams for six months.

"David?" My voice comes out as a whisper, unworthy of a stage actress.

He steps inside, hands tucked into the pockets of his jeans. He's wearing a suit jacket over a simple t-shirt, dressed up but not too formal. The sight of him knocks the wind out of me. He's more beautiful than I remembered, and I remembered him as practically perfect.

"Hey." His lips curve into a smile that crinkles the corners of his eyes. "Whitney Barnes, Broadway sensation."

I'm on my feet before I realize what I'm doing, crossing the small space between us in three quick steps. My arms find their way around him, pulling him close, *and God,* he feels the same. Solid and warm and real. My face presses against his chest, and I breathe him in—cologne and laundry detergent and something uniquely David.

His arms wrap around me, holding tight, and for a moment, we just stand there. I'm trembling, and I can feel his heart racing under my cheek. When he finally lets go, I have to force myself to step back.

"What are you doing here?" I ask, searching his face. "How did you—when did you—"

"Quinn told me you were in another show." He shrugs, but his eyes never leave mine. "I figured it was time I came to see what all the fuss was about."

"And?"

"And you were amazing." The sincerity in his voice makes my knees weak. "Though I have to say, I was a little jealous of that actor who got to kiss you in the second act."

I laugh, and it feels like the first real laugh I've had in months. "That's Jackson. He's gay and engaged to the most gorgeous man you've ever seen."

"Good." David grins. "Because I'm not sure I could handle competition right now."

My heart skips at the implication. "Competition?"

He takes a step closer, reaching out to tuck a strand of hair behind my ear. The touch of his fingers against my skin sends electricity racing down my spine.

"I tried, Whitney. I really did. I tried to forget you. Tried to convince myself that what we had was just physical. That I could find it with someone else." His voice drops lower. "But no one else is you."

"David..."

"Let me finish." He takes a deep breath. "I graduate in December. I've been offered a job at an engineering firm here in New York. Starting in January."

The words hit me like a thunderbolt, and I struggle to process what he's saying. "You're... *moving* to New York?"

"I'm moving to New York," he confirms. "And I know you've got your career, and I've got mine, and maybe this is crazy, but I couldn't stop thinking about what might have happened if we'd given us a real chance."

"I was scared," I admit, the words tumbling out before I can stop them. "I thought I had to choose—my dream or love. I didn't know how to have both."

"And now?"

"Now I think maybe the dream isn't complete without someone to share it with."

David's smile grows wider, and he takes both my hands in his. "When Quinn told me you were here, I knew I had to see you. I had to know if what we had was real or if I'd built it up in my head."

"And?"

"And the moment I saw you on that stage, I knew. It *was* real. It is real." He squeezes my hands. "Six months is a long time, Whitney. But some things don't change."

I feel tears threatening, but I blink them back. "Like what?"

He leans in, his forehead touching mine, his breath warm against my lips. "Like the fact that I'm completely, utterly in love with you. Have been since that first night, when you were still Nikki and I was still Jax."

The words wash over me, healing something I didn't know was broken. I reach up, cupping his face in my hands, overwhelmed by how right this feels—him, here, in my world.

"I love you too," I whisper. "I think I always have."

David's smile is brighter than any spotlight I've ever stood under. "I was hoping you'd say that. Because I didn't come all this way just to watch your play."

"No?"

"No." He pulls me closer, his arms encircling my waist. "I came to ask the most talented, beautiful, complicated woman I know if she might want to try something new."

"What's that?" I ask, though I already know the answer.

"A relationship. A *real* one. No fake names, no holding back. Just us, figuring it out together."

I smile, feeling lighter than I have in months. "I think I'd like that."

"Good." David brushes his lips against mine, soft and sweet and full of promise. "Because I've got tickets to your show for the next three nights, and I plan to be front row center for all of them."

THE END

Acknowledgments

"Make You Mine"
Artist . 🎵 . Madison Beer
Written by Beer and Leroy Clampitt

"Express Yourself"
Artist . 🎵 . Madonna
Written by Madonna and Stephen Bray

Los Angeles, California

Manhattan, New York

You Might Also Like

Love Child - Part 1

Trixi Matthews had always known who her biological father was. Her mother had been a maid in the wealthy businessman's household for years, and Mr. Fischer frequently took advantage of her mother's youth.

Twenty-four years later, Trixi now wants to know him. At first, stalking Mr. Fischer had been easy - she had easily gone unnoticed until she's discovered by the covert operations of his wayward son.

Grayson Fischer had noticed her from the start! Trixi was unlike any girl he'd ever seen - but who was she really?

They meet by chance, and Trixi keeps her secret ... until Grayson begins to show his feelings for her. Find out what happens when the mystery gets revealed.

Part 1 of 2

BWWM Romance

Ebook & Paperback

Love Child - Part 2

Grayson Fischer cannot believe his horrible fate. He's found the woman of his dreams—but she turns out to be his half-sister? What hellish nightmare was this?

Trixi Matthews finally gets to know her biological father, it's all she's ever dreamed of, but her feelings for Grayson make her lovesick with the understanding of the truth.

What happens to Trixi and Grayson? Do they give into their twisted attraction to one another? Or do they go their separate ways, and face eternal heartbreak?

Find out what happens in Part Two of "Love Child - A BWWM Romance"

Part 2 of 2

A BWWM Romance

Ebook & Paperback

New for 2025

Paris Fling

Love is a Parisian Adventure

Single mom finds love in the City of Lights, but will her daughter's wild night complicate things?

In Dylan Roxi's hilarious BWWM romance comedy, Tanya's world gets turned upside down when her fiercely independent single mom, Shaniece, announces she's getting married...in Paris! Determined to stop this whirlwind romance, Tanya jets off to France, only to get swept up in her own unexpected Parisian fling.

Will Tanya sabotage her mom's happiness? Can a one-night stand turn into more?

A BWWM Romance

Available in

Ebook & Paperback

About Dylan

Dylan Roxi is an emerging author of BWWM Romance and Contemporary Modern Fiction. Dylan has many writing interests and lives an incognito digital lifestyle.

Dylan is part of the Ardent Artist Books family and is the author of several published books.

amazon.com/Ardent-Artist-Books/e/B08BX8F1DZ
youtube.com/theardentartist

Also by Dylan

Love Child - Part 1

Love Child - Part 2

Offsides

Almost Yours

Cougar at Play

Paris Fling

Dorm Room 2B or Not 2B

www.ingramcontent.com/pod-product-compliance
Lightning Source LLC
LaVergne TN
LVHW081813080526
838199LV00099B/4327